BMX
TUNNEL RUN

D1374284

Pam Withers

WALRUS
B O O K S

Edited by Carolyn Bateman
Proofread by Joan Templeton
Cover and interior design by Roberta Batchelor
Cover photograph by Kevin Saborit
Typeset by Jesse Marchand

Printed and bound in Canada

Library and Archives Canada Cataloguing in Publication

Withers, Pam

   BMX tunnel run / Pam Withers.

(Take it to the Extreme)

ISBN 978-1-55285-904-9

ISBN 1-55285-904-5

   I. Title. II. Series: Withers, Pam. Take it to the Extreme.

PS8595.I8453B59 2007   jC813'.6   C2007-901775-4

The publisher acknowledges the financial support of the Canada Council for the Arts, the British Columbia Arts Council, and the Government of Canada through the Book Publishing Industry Development Program (BPIDP). Whitecap Books also acknowledges the financial support of the Province of British Columbia through the Book Publishing Tax Credit.

 Canada Council Conseil des Arts
for the Arts   du Canada
        BRITISH COLUMBIA
       ARTS COUNCIL

The inside pages of this book are 100% recycled, processed chlorine-free paper with 40% post-consumer content. For more information, visit Markets Initiative's website: www.oldgrowthfree.com.

 ANCIENT FOREST
FRIENDLY

Dedicated to Terry's grandchildren:
James, David, Michael, Nicola, Sarah, and Alanah

Contents

1 The Maze

Jake Evans gripped the handlebars of his BMX bike tightly and leaned into the sharp curve.

"Noooo!" he protested as his tires made it around a blind U-turn, and a dead end threatened to imprint itself on his face. He squeezed the brakes and prepared for contact as he felt himself hurled over the handlebars.

The body-jarring landing knocked the wind out of him. Dust filled his nostrils as he struggled to suck in air. He'd landed like a dead beetle, face and legs up to the clear blue sky, buttocks against a cornstalk that blockaded the path. Bits of gravel on the narrow, dirty trail pressed into his bare back.

As he lay there breathing hard, a crackling sound overhead startled him. Then something hard fell through the air and landed on his gut like a light punch. He lifted his chin and closed a hand around it.

"Corn on the cob," he announced to a chickadee that had just perched itself on the stalk tops high above him. "If you have to crash a bike, at least a cornfield is softer than concrete."

He peeled the coarse husk away from the cob and examined the pale yellow corn. "Nope, not ripe. Anyway, I prefer 'em cooked and buttered."

He tossed the cob away, into the shadows of the thick forest of stalks that surrounded him. The bird twittered and flapped away.

"Hey," he called to it. "Come back and tell me how to get out of here."

Corn mazes had always intrigued Jake, and he'd been totally into it when his best buddy Peter Montpetit had suggested they sneak into this one and bike its labyrinth of paths before the site opened to the public at four o'clock.

Only trouble was, mazes were about getting a person lost, and he'd been lost for half an hour. He sighed and spun his undamaged bike around. "Peter," he called. "I'm lost!"

Only the rasp of grasshoppers and chirp of crickets responded. That meant either Peter had long since found his way to the finish or was pretending he couldn't hear Jake to make sure he'd win their little race. The last time Peter got lost in a maze, Jake remembered, his friend had wriggled his way through a hedge to find a new corridor. Typical Peter: an impulsive, quick-thinking kind of guy. The correct way to get out of a maze, Jake figured, was to stay calm and focused.

Ten minutes later, having managed to avoid further dead ends, Jake reached the stairs that led up to the maze's viewing platform. "Yes!" he said as he did a happy nose manual.

Seven steps to the platform. Hmmm. Perfect for a skilled flatlander—a BMXer who's into tricks that demand balance and control. He placed his feet on his pedals, stood on them, and began a warm-up bouncing while parallel to the steps. One, two, three, JUMP! Step number two was now his. One, two, three, JUMP! And so it went. Jake teetered once or twice as he attained a new step, but never faltered, fell, or needed to take his feet off the pedals.

The juice in his calves was burning as he made the last leap onto the deck.

"What took you so long, old buddy? And do you plan to pogo the steps down without casing your back tire?"

Jake grinned as he dropped his bike and punched Peter lightly in the shoulder. "Ha!" he replied. "Up here scouting? Nice to know I'm not the only one lost."

"Lost? No way. Just hanging out enjoying the view,"

Peter protested. "Want half an apple?" he asked, producing one from his pocket.

"Sure."

"Think I'm strong enough to break it in half with my bare hands?"

"Is this another one of your stupid magic tricks?" Jake had been subjected to Peter's bumbling attempts at being the next Houdini for a couple of weeks now. It was Peter's new obsession, aside from BMX biking.

Ignoring the taunt, Peter held the apple up for Jake to inspect. It was a normal apple, no cuts, no marks of any kind.

"One, two, three, voila." Peter cupped the apple between his palms, then twisted each palm an opposite way. The apple broke in two pieces, the break as clean as if a sharp knife had cut it.

"Wanna know how I did that?" Peter asked, gloating as he handed one half to Jake.

"You're not supposed to tell how you do magic tricks."

Peter shrugged. "I stuck a threaded needle under the skin by the stem, then down, then along the bottom, then back up and across, like a square. Then I pulled on the two ends of the thread. That sliced it inside without breaking the skin except for the needle holes. Cool, huh?"

"Cool," Jake allowed. "Houdini teach you that?"

"Houdini the master magician did way cooler things. But hey, I'm still a beginner. I'll get to Houdini tricks one of these days."

"Houdini wouldn't have gotten lost in this maze."

"You got that right," Peter said, straightening up and looking off into the distance. "Can you see my cabin from here?"

Jake shaded his eyes and turned slowly around. To the south of the maze were endless fields of corn, hay, cows, and chicken sheds. To the north were the shacks and rundown houses of Copperton, British Columbia—shadowed by rugged, stony hills with patches of trees and grass. They were about 300 miles northeast of Seattle, Peter's home. Between the hills and small town was a lake dotted by summer cabins.

"You mean your parents' cabin, which they're up here to sell?" Jake responded. It was kind of a mean thing to say, but Jake was worried about how Peter wasn't really facing up to that fact. Jake and Peter had grown up next door to each other and were still best of friends now, at age fifteen. That was despite Peter's airplane-pilot dad getting a high-paying job about the same time as Jake's family had fallen on hard times a few years back. Since then, Jake had gotten used to Peter having fancy vacations, expensive sports gear, and a huge allowance. And lately, Peter had switched to a private school. But Peter's carefree approach to money and his lack of sensitivity toward people with less often bugged Jake. In fact, Jake was beginning to think Peter was becoming even more of a snob as he tried to deny that his own family's situation had just taken an abrupt turn. Peter's mom and dad had both been laid off for a few months now, were struggling financially for the first time in their lives, and had decided to try and sell the property.

"Okay, my parents' cabin. But they're not really going to sell it, so don't even say that," Peter insisted.

Jake nodded, deciding not to push things. "Yeah, I see your cabin. Hey, nearly as many cabins on Copper Lake as houses in Copperton."

"Yeah, and that's good, 'cause it gives work to the locals."

"Uh-huh," Jake responded. "You mean like the $10 we just cheated this farmer out of?"

"Well, we could've waited till the maze opened and then paid to walk it, but that would've been boring. Way more fun to sneak in and bike it, hey?"

Jake shrugged. "Let's go bike the track." He meant, of course, the local BMX racetrack. They'd been at the lake for a week. Hadn't taken them long to check out almost everything in the little town, but they hadn't actually biked on the track yet.

"I've told you the locals never let us lake kids on it," Peter grumped. "We'll just have to build dirt jumps somewhere, maybe tomorrow. Ready to go home now?"

"Sounds good to me," Jake agreed. He preferred dirt jumps to racetracks anyway. Speed on racetracks was Peter's thing. Jumping wide gaps on dirt jumps was Jake's thing.

"Are you starting to get bored here already?" Peter asked Jake.

Jake hesitated, hoping it wouldn't be rude to answer that honestly. Then he grinned. "Yeah, a little. It'd be nice if there were something exciting to do besides bike around."

Peter sighed. "Something exciting. I agree. As if that's possible in Copperton." He looked down from their bridge. "So, about this maze. Looks like if we take a right at the bottom of these steps, then four lefts, two rights, and two lefts, we'll be out!"

The two bumped their bikes down the steps, peeled right, and did a high-speed chase to the maze's exit without getting lost again.

Peter won, of course. "Guess you didn't eat your Wheaties for breakfast this morning."

"Yeah? Let's hear you say that when we get some jumps built," Jake teased back as they headed toward Peter's cabin. Their route had them skirting the town, past the town dump, and up a blacktop road to the lake. Before they reached the blacktop, something caught Jake's eye: a glint of metal at the edge of the dump. As he biked closer, it came into fuller view.

"Hey, Peter, stop for a second. Look at this." Jake turned left off the road to bike a few yards up the dump's driveway. And there he saw an old-school Norco BMX bike at the edge of the mountain of garbage. Peter braked to a stop beside him.

"Kinda old and rusty," Peter said, "but not worth tossing. Sure stinks here," he added, nose wrinkled. "Only hick towns have open dumps like this. Hmmm, someone used to race this bike. Still has a number plate. Anyway, we could take it if we put it between our bikes and each held onto a handle."

"Good idea."

"Not a good idea," boomed a voice from somewhere in the trash. "Get lost. That's mine!"

Jake swung around to see a boy their age in camouflage trousers, filthy T-shirt, and a buzz cut. He was small and wiry, but looked tough. And his jaw was set as hard as his eyes.

"Sorry," Jake started to say, eyes shifting to the boy's hold on a big cardboard box marked "military" that he'd dug out of the trash heap.

"Like we'd know it's yours if it's leaning up against a pile of garbage," Peter called out. "Anyway, we're outta here. Come on, Jake."

2   Copperton

They reached Peter's cabin breathing hard from a fast ride.

"That guy was a jerk," Peter muttered.

"He was just stopping us from stealing his bike," Jake suggested.

"They're all like that around here," Peter said. "The locals hate us. They're mostly mining families, rednecks. Got great big chips on their shoulders, especially since the mine here closed."

"So there used to be a mine here? I thought Copperton was an army base," Jake said.

"Most of the mine closed thirty years ago. Parts were still going till ten years ago. The army base closed a few months back. So Copperton is kind of dying, except for weekends and summers when people come to the lake." Peter's hand swept the air, gesturing at all the cabins. "Copperton people need us, but they don't like us. And they think we're all rich."

"I suppose you are compared with them," Jake said. He couldn't say "we are," since his family probably wasn't much better off than the unemployed mining and military families in Copperton. "People who buy cabins make land prices go up, drive flashy cars, and are always on vacation. That's all the locals are thinking."

"Oh yeah? How would you know what Copperton people are thinking? My family has been here for years, Jake. Trust me, the hicks around here don't want to talk to us, never have. Won't share their racetrack, either." He eyed a tree and accelerated toward it. Jake knew he was going for a tree tap, maybe to burn off tension. Jake watched as Peter ran his front wheel partway up the tree, then leaped his bike back to the ground, his feet never leaving his pedals.

Jake knew better than to argue further. He was Peter's guest for a few weeks, after all. But he couldn't help thinking: Just you wait, Peter. If your mom and dad don't get jobs soon, you'll learn to stop calling people with less money "hicks."

"Hi, Dad," Peter greeted his father, who was kneeling on the front steps of the cabin with a screwdriver applied to a plate above the doorknob. "Whatcha up to?"

"Hi, son. Hi, Jake," Richard Montpetit said without looking up. "Replacing the locks."

"How come?" Peter asked as he and Jake dropped their bikes and started up the front steps.

"Old ones weren't very strong. And looks better for resale value."

Jake watched Peter's face dim. His buddy was definitely in denial about the whole cabin-sale issue, if not about both his parents having lost their jobs. His mom was a flight attendant.

"Anyone who really wants to get in can get in," Peter asserted. "Houdini once picked handcuff locks that a blacksmith spent five years designing. They were supposed to be totally pick-proof."

There he goes again, thought Jake. Two months ago, after seeing a movie about Houdini's life, Peter had entered into a phase of studying magic tricks and famous magicians. Being athletic, he was especially into magicians who specialized in feats involving contortion or physical endurance. Jake suspected it was Peter's way of escaping the tension his family was going through lately.

Mr. Montpetit sat back on his haunches and smiled. "Good thing the closest thing to Houdini in Copperton is you, son. And to tell you the truth, I don't mind if you two do a disappearing act between now and supper so I can finish this."

"No problem. Can I have a couple of dollars for some ice cream?"

Jake watched Peter's dad frown. "Peter, you've been told no allowance this summer. That means no money for treats, either."

"Hey, I'll bring you home your favorite sundae," Peter coaxed.

But Peter's dad was back concentrating on the lock. "Nice try, son. Scram, you two."

Peter, smile undimmed, shrugged his shoulders, jingled some coins in his shorts pocket, and jerked his head toward town. "I'm buying, Jake. Race you there."

"I'll buy my own," Jake objected as the two jumped on their BMXs, did a bunny hop each, and sped down the hill. It was one thing for Peter to treat him when Peter had money, but Jake didn't like the way his friend was acting as if his savings weren't draining away.

Of course, Peter could always sell one of his bikes, Jake reasoned. He had two: one for dirt jumps and street riding, which he was using today, and one for racing. Both were way more expensive than Jake could afford. The one Peter was on now had forty-eight triple-walled spokes, pegs of aluminum-wrapped titanium, and steel forks. Built piece by piece in Germany.

Jake sighed. His own was a made-in-China stock dirt-jump bike with a slightly bent rim that he'd bought second hand. But unlike Peter, Jake had a knack for fixing things; people often said he was just like his mechanic dad. Anyway, Jake was saving up for chromoly forks. Then he'd upgrade his brake system, maybe get better pegs, too.

Jake hardly ever raced because he didn't have a racing bike. Peter, of course, had a sweet sixteen-pounder with carbon forks and cassette hubs. No wonder he won lots of races, though the truth was, Peter was fast on any bike. He was a fast kind of guy. Fast and stubborn, Jake reflected with a frown. And grumpy lately. No way would Peter admit he shouldn't be buying ice cream in town. But Jake would go along with it, if only because he didn't feel like arguing with Peter these days, given his family troubles. Plus, it was a hot day and a cone would go down really well right now.

"Double scoop of chocolate chip mint in a waffle cone and whatever my buddy wants," Peter was saying ten minutes later to the tall, muscular, dark-haired boy behind the counter.

"Single scoop of chocolate in a regular cone, please," Jake said.

Peter could've said please, Jake thought as he watched a scowl across the server boy's face deepen above an angry-looking, purple chin scar. Jake wanted to object to Peter paying, but the money was in the server's hand before Jake could open his mouth. The boy, who looked their age, rammed his ice cream scooper deep into the bucket, his impressive biceps rippling with the effort. He slopped two balls into a cone without once meeting Peter's eyes, then shoved the cone at him like it was a boxing glove doing a fake punch.

Peter gave Jake a sideways wink and headed for an empty table.

The server moved to the chocolate ice cream bucket. "Single, you said?" he barked without looking at Jake.

"Yes, in a regular cone," Jake responded. "Hot today, eh? Is it always this hot around here?"

The boy's wrist paused for a split second, and his narrowed eyes swept quickly over Jake before returning to the ice cream. He shrugged.

"Hey, I was wondering about the BMX track," Jake said, speaking cheerfully and looking directly at the athletic-looking boy. "Any chance visitors can bike it? We're BMXers."

The boy directed a hard stare at Jake, flicked his eyes to Peter and back. Then he handed Jake his ice cream cone and wiped his hands on a wet cloth. "Locals only," he grunted. He turned abruptly, then nodded to a boy entering from the back room with a broom in hand.

"Hey Russell, you're late," the server said. "I'm taking my break now."

The sweeper looked familiar to Jake.

"Okay, Micah. I'm late 'cause I found something real good at the dump. Tell you later," he said in a lowered voice.

Jake suddenly realized it was the boy they'd almost stolen the bike from at the dump.

"Racetrack after work?" Russell was asking Micah, his voice hesitant.

"Maybe," Micah said as he strode off through an "employees only" door without so much as a backward glance at Jake, Peter, or Russell.

Jake swiveled quickly before Russell could recognize him and joined Peter.

"See what I mean?" Peter said. "No point trying to ride at their track, and no point trying to be friendly. It's them and us in this town. Totally stupid, but that's the way it is. Hey, isn't that the dumpster diver behind the counter?"

"Shhh," Jake hushed him, embarrassed by Peter's words and tone.

But he needn't have worried. Peter was too into his ice cream to follow up the comment.

"Mmmm, chocolate chip mint," Peter murmured.

"Mmmm, a BMX race," Jake responded.

"Huh?"

"That sign on the bulletin board over there. Says there's a BMX race here—this weekend."

"A BMX race in Copperton? You're kidding. Never been one here before. Who'd come for it?" He stood and walked briskly over to the poster. "Seriously! Sweet! Okay, they have to let us enter," he enthused. "We'll kick—"

"We? You mean you, Peter. But only if you get that front wheel trued on your racing bike first. I can do it if we get a spoke wrench somewhere."

"Now, that's a deal!" Peter all but shouted. "You're good for another cone!" He dug his hand into his shorts pocket, brought out a handful of change and a few bills, and frowned. "Sure I can't ride my race bike like it is?"

He clearly had enough money for another cone, but Jake was glad to see him being careful rather than spending everything he had. "No way you can ride on a warped wheel and loose spokes. Anyway, I don't want more ice cream. I can straighten that wheel and save you having to buy a new rim and rebuild the wheel. You shouldn't be spending that kind of money. The point is, you're going to own that race."

3   Locals

A race right here in Copperton while Jake and I are on vacation, Peter mused. How cool is that? Maybe Jake could borrow a bike and enter the race, too. And maybe I can win and get some money to put toward new forks.

It was a major bummer not getting allowance anymore. His parents were being real tightwads considering this was summer vacation. He and Jake wouldn't start their summer jobs for a few weeks yet, but at least then they'd have some money. Peter refused to worry between now and then; he could always borrow from his dad if he got short. And a good set of forks on his racing bike was an essential, not a luxury.

"Hardware store is only two blocks from the ice cream shop," Peter informed Jake as they passed a boarded-up army supplies store. The place had closed when the local base had shut down. No great loss as far as Peter was concerned.

"No bike shop?" Jake asked.

Peter laughed. "This is a hick town, remember? The place we're going is a hardware store, bike shop, and locksmith all in one. Which reminds me, I need new locks to practice picking. Wonder if they have handcuffs, too," he joked. "I could use a second pair."

Jake rolled his eyes, but Peter made a mental note to mail-order some more handcuffs over the Internet.

"Houdini was the best lock picker ever. He was also an acrobat at nine years old, you know," Peter informed Jake. Peter loved reading about Houdini and the modern-day Houdini, David Blaine. They made him forget everything around him, especially his parents who were so grumpy and tense lately. Magic tricks made him feel powerful.

"I know. You've told me a hundred times. And he ran away from home at twelve, and was the greatest escape artist in the world."

"'Cause he practiced all the time," Peter reminded Jake, feeling defensive as usual when his buddy took no interest in what had become his favorite subject. "Used to hold his breath underwater in his bathtub, longer each time, till his lungs got really strong."

"Your lungs are the strongest ones I know, if talking a lot counts," Jake teased back. "Guess this is the hardware store," he added as they pulled up. "Do me a favor and don't ask if they have handcuffs."

At least Jake was smiling when he said it. Well, Peter thought, it took Houdini a while to get respect, too. He paused after they locked their bikes up on the rack outside the store. Something was different about the hardware store, he judged. Used to be, well, gray and rundown, run by an old man who looked like he should've retired years earlier. Someone had repainted it red and put in window displays. And there was a lineup of BMX bikes just inside. And a sign, "Rental bikes available!!" Yes, two exclamation marks after it.

"Hello there!" enthused a smiling man behind the counter as the boys entered the shop. "Where are you visiting from and what can I do for you today? I'm Greg Lowe, the new owner."

A local who's friendly? Peter thought. And he talks like he just finished a marketing course.

"Staying in a cabin up at the lake," Jake said. "Came in for a spoke wrench. For a BMX racing bike."

"No kidding. Both you boys BMXers?"

"Yes," Peter replied. "Know anything about a BMX race here Saturday?"

The middle-aged man had a baby face and a balding head topped by tufts of red hair that looked windblown. He stood behind the counter with a goofy smile on his face. A super nerd, Peter thought, amused. The guy stepped out from behind the cash register and extended his hand to each of the boys for a shake. *A store owner is shaking our hands? In Copperton?*

"I know lots about it, since I organized it. My daughter Kasey is really into BMXing," Mr. Lowe boasted. "She wins most of her races, even gets asked for autographs by the other girls." His chest puffed out a little.

"A racer, a girl racer," Peter mused aloud. *A girl racer with a weird, motormouth dad who seems to worship her.* He turned toward Jake in time to catch him trying not to smile.

"She's also an amazing singer. Even gets paid to sing sometimes," Mr. Lowe said, nodding his smiling head like one of those bobbing figures that people put on their car dashboards.

"Yeah? What'd you say her name was?" Peter asked. *If there really was a big-name BMX racer in Copperton, that'd be cool, not that he cared whether she could sing.* But just for fun, he formed an image of his favorite female pop singer—long blonde hair and well built, of course—slinging a leg over a BMX bike and winking at him before clearing a high-speed triple jump.

"Kasey with a 'K.' Kasey Lowe. She's fourteen. My wife died two years ago and we moved to Copperton to start again, if you know what I mean. I like this place. I'm keen to make a go of it."

Poor guy, thought Peter. And poor 'Kasey with a K.' He'd never heard of her, though he didn't know the Canadian racers that well. "Cool. Well, like we said, we came in here to buy a spoke wrench," Peter reminded the wacky hardware store owner.

"So do you have to live in Copperton to enter the race?" Jake asked.

"Of course not! Hoping to get lots of racers from all over. I organized it to help Kasey make friends, and maybe get the store known better, too."

"Great," Jake said. "But only locals are allowed on the track till race day?"

"Oh, there's a few kids around who think that. But if you boys want to use it, go right on ahead. Don't let a few spoilsports put you off."

"Alright! We certainly won't!" Peter said. "Maybe we can even get your daughter to coach us." Why not play along with the dad's boastfulness about his daughter?

"Excellent idea! She'd probably love to. So what kind of wrench this afternoon?"

Peter selected and paid for the wrench, which cost a little more than he'd hoped, but didn't use up all the money he had on him. Then he noticed Jake busy talking with Mr. Lowe about bike repairs. So

Peter chose some inexpensive locks to play with, then started cruising the aisles, looking for other stuff he could work into a magic show.

He wasn't going to be an ordinary magician. No way. He was into training to be a contortionist, someone fit enough to survive difficult feats, like Houdini or Blaine. Blaine once had himself frozen into the middle of a block of ice. He stayed like that for three days and three nights. He started to hallucinate, but he was still alive at the end of the three days. You had to be fit for stuff like that, had to be strong and clever and keep a cool head. Once, Peter remembered, Houdini had jumped off a bridge in handcuffs and chains. As people along shore had gasped, he'd reappeared, totally free, in fifteen seconds. What a man!

"Ready to go?" Jake was asking as Peter checked out the price for chains and decided to hold off for now.

"Hey, here's Kasey," Mr. Lowe called out. "Jake—and your friend's name is Peter? Come meet my daughter. Kasey, these boys are from the lake, and they have BMX bikes."

"You guys ride?" a short, pudgy girl with the frizziest red hair Peter had ever seen stood with her hands on her hips near the counter. She was wearing a bright pink track suit and red runners, and her red-freckled face looked at them suspiciously. There was certainly no hint of a welcome.

Okay, Peter thought, definitely no resemblance to my favorite pop star. Oh well. Wonder if she can really ride?

"Yes," Jake replied for both of them, "we ride."

Kasey tossed her shoulder-length hair, which sort of bounced in response, and she took a last sip from the bottle of flavored mineral water she was holding. As she set it down on the counter, her father jumped up and hurried to carry it away, like he was a waiter and she was an important customer.

"Honey, I'm going into the back for a minute, okay? Nice to meet you boys." He nodded to them and moved through a door to some back rooms.

Jake was saying to Kasey, "So we were hoping to check out some trails up in the hills tomorrow."

"You think?" It sounded like a challenge. She was looking the boys up and down like they were merchandise she needed to tag. She tossed her mane of hair again. "Kind of rocky there. Not great for your bikes."

"Maybe the racetrack, then?" Peter suggested, testing her.

She turned and scrutinized him. "Sorry, only locals are allowed on the track."

"But your dad said ..." Peter began.

"Don't believe anything my dad says, especially about me," she replied, her face reddening to the point that her freckles almost disappeared. Then she paused. "You race? What're your names again?"

"Jake Evans," Jake said. "We just came in to buy a wrench."

"Oh." Kasey nodded curtly and looked at Peter in that resentful, unfriendly way that the local kids here always looked at the lake kids.

"Peter Montpetit," Peter said, wondering how he and Jake could change her mind about using the track. He watched her face go red for a second time as she stared at him, her eyes going wide.

"Peter Montpetit from Seattle?"

Peter was startled for a second. He was sure he'd never seen her before. "Yeah, I'm from Seattle."

The redhead dropped her hands from her hips. Her mouth hung open a little and her eyebrows went arched. She came out from behind the counter and twisted her hands in front of her.

"You, um, raced in the nationals last year, right? And you got three firsts and one third in Washington state this year?"

"Uh, yeah." Huh? She read Washington race results? But she certainly wouldn't be impressed by that if she were really good herself.

"Kasey Lowe," she said, extending her hand a little shyly. "Would you consider riding in our little week-end race? I assume Dad told you about it. I hate to think what he said. He is so embarrassing." She gave a little nervous giggle. "I mean, our event isn't much, but that'd be so cool if you could. And your friend too. Jake Evans?" she asked, turning to smile at Jake, who was looking at her with the same mystified face as Peter.

"Ah, sure. We were planning to enter," Peter said, accepting her handshake. "But you were saying there's no way to practice on the course beforehand?" What was with this girl? One minute she's an ice queen with the we-hate-weekenders glare, and now she's Copperton's Welcome Wagon rep? Peter was no hot-shot by anyone's standards, so it made no sense for her to have changed personalities so suddenly.

"Uh, sorry about that." She hung her head and her freckles disappeared yet again. "There are these guys in town who made that rule. And I'm kind of new here, so it's what I'm supposed to say." She looked at Peter, then Jake, with an appeal for understanding. "They'll chase you off if I'm not there. But if you go when I go …"

"Really?" Jake interrupted in an innocent-sounding voice. "Why's that?"

"'Cause my dad owns this store and I get them discounts on tools and bike parts," she explained, crossing her arms for a second, then hurriedly uncrossing them as if eager not to offend. "So they have to be nice to me. Anyway, I train there most afternoons around two o'clock if you're interested. Maybe the day after tomorrow?"

"Sure. Thanks," Peter said. What luck, being allowed on the course by this newcomer to town, never mind what strange reasons she had for changing her mind. The way she'd first talked to them, he'd figured she thought as highly of herself as her dad did of her. And her dad was seriously over the top. Seemed to think his daughter was on the brink of becoming a superstar at something. Well, if his wife had died two years ago, it wouldn't be too surprising if he focused way too much attention on his daughter. But she had said, "Don't believe anything my dad says, especially about me."

Maybe she was their key to biking good stuff around here. Odd as she was, she was way friendlier than other kids in Copperton. Which didn't take much, he concluded with a grin.

"So you're an awesome singer and a star racer, we hear," Peter ventured.

Kasey's hands flew to her face, where she squeezed them into fists. "I'll kill him if he keeps saying that," she said. "He actually said that to you?"

"Nah, I'm exaggerating. No worries. So how long've you been in Copperton?" Peter asked.

"Six months. I like it except there's not many kids. Hard to make friends," she said, shrugging.

"I like Copperton. It's a cool little place," Jake offered.

Peter watched Kasey eye Jake like she was measuring whether he was joking. She stuffed her hands into her pockets, then pulled them out and looked at the door as the shop bell rang to signify that a customer had entered. "Yeah, well, see you around. Maybe at the racetrack," she said. She did a little nervous wave to them before turning to the new customer and saying, "How can I help you?"

"So, you have a fan in Copperton," Jake needled Peter as they rode toward the cabin a few minutes later, with the new wrench in Jake's pack. "Thought she was going to ask you for your autograph there for a second. And there goes your theory about locals hating weekenders."

"Fan? She's just weird," Peter protested. "And her dad's even weirder. But she's going to let us on the racetrack. Can't argue with that."

"True," Jake agreed, grinning.

"So, let's hit the hills and find a secret place to build jumps tomorrow, I say. Then see if we can really get on the racetrack the next day."

"I'd definitely be into that," Jake agreed.

4   Abandoned Mine

Jake wasn't sure what he expected from the hills above the lake, but if he and Peter were looking for loose dirt somewhere hidden from sight, it didn't look good. All he could see were rock-strewn hills with occasional bits of green—strange little hillocks in the shadow of more natural-looking hills. Piles of rock cluttered the occasional cliff base, and waist-high grass pressed around cellar holes of former houses with lonely, crumbling chimneys. When Jake biked up alongside one of these foundations and peered into it, he saw a rusty, overturned stove and shards of broken glass.

"Did this used to be part of Copperton?" Jake asked Peter. "Looks like a ghost town." He noticed one house intact except for its sagging porch, broken windows, and peeling paint. A "no trespassing" sign was nailed across the door.

"Nah, this is what's left of the mine," Peter informed him. "Those funny little hills are actually mine tailings, the stuff left over from all the digging. And there used to be a village of miners' houses here. Follow me. I'll show you something else."

Jake's feet pumped his pedals to follow Peter around a hillock, where both stopped dead. Whoa, now there was a sight. A massive industrial building, or what was left of it, maybe eight stories high, built against a slope. Rusty pipes and twisted metal rails stuck out of it, and barbed-wire fencing surrounded it. Even from where they'd paused, Jake could see a dozen signs warning, "Danger. Do not enter. No trespassing."

"That's the biggest building still standing. Dad says that's where they sorted the rocks they hauled up from underground."

"Sorted them for what?" Jake wondered.

"For the ones with copper in them, I guess. No, wait. For the ones with minerals in them that they shipped off to some giant furnace that turned them into copper. This used to be one of the biggest copper mines in the world, I heard."

"Oh. So are there mine tunnels under us?" Jake asked his buddy, looking nervously at a sort of sinkhole beside the trail they were on.

"Lots of them." Peter's eyes followed Jake's to the

sinkhole. "But they've all been sealed up. Once when we were here in winter I saw steam coming out of that crater. Must be an old mine shaft. Cool, isn't it?"

"Sure is, but where are we going to build dirt jumps?" Jake asked, eyes scanning the rubble.

"Follow me."

Jake cranked his pedals and wound his way up some more hillocks. The old mine workings spoiled the scenery a little, but the air smelled fresh up here, and the sun felt warm on his face. Small rocks crunched under the tread of his tires with a sort of musical beat. He didn't even mind the way the handle of the shovel he carried in his backpack kept bumping the back of his neck. He nodded approvingly when Peter led them into a thin grove of trees.

"Perfect," he agreed as they dismounted and shed their backpacks in a clearing. The ground was still rocky, but it was doable. There was a peek-a-boo view of some of the former mine buildings from here. They peeled their sweaty shirts off and started digging, packing, and shaping the dirt. They'd been at it a hard fifteen minutes when movement up the hill caught the corner of Jake's eye.

"Hey," he notified Peter as he put his shovel down. "Riders."

"Hmmm," Peter said in a low voice, eyes following Jake's between the trees and up the hill. "Looks like

Copperton's entire BMX team. There's Mr. Ice Cream Server …"

"Micah," Jake corrected him.

"And the dumpster diver, and the girl champ."

"Russell and Kasey," Jake whispered, annoyed at Peter's sarcasm. "Bet they know the best trails up here. Let's watch where they go. Or maybe they'd even be into helping us build jumps—"

"Jake, don't be stupid. They wouldn't help build them. They'd just wreck them. Why do you think I chose somewhere in the trees? How many times do I have to tell you they're locals, Jake? That means jerks."

Jake shook his head but didn't reply. Instead, he moved to the edge of the grove and watched the three youths race along the rim of a hillock before yahooing, catching some air, and disappearing over the horizon. Pretty good riders, he thought. And that looks like a good jump.

"I'm checking out that jump," he said, grabbing his bike.

"Jake," Peter started to object, but a minute later, Jake could hear Peter pedaling hard to catch up. Jake headed straight for the place he'd last seen the group. Sure enough, there was a nice flat stretch to work up speed just before a drop-off down an angled dirt slope. It provided a sweet-looking leap for sure. Breathing hard, Jake sprinted for the ledge, cleared it, and did a quick Superman. Hands gripping his handlebars, he lifted his legs and body straight out behind him for a split second. As the wind whistled past his ears, he smiled, then landed his bike like a pro and braked to a halt right before some sharp rocks that looked eager to eat his tires.

He moved to make way for Peter's smooth landing nearby, then scanned the open, rock-strewn hillside and scratched his head. "Where'd they go? No place to hide here."

"I don't get it," Peter agreed, looking equally confused.

They looked left, right, straight ahead, and even back up the slope. No one. But there was no way the three could have gotten out of sight in the short time it had taken the boys to reach the ledge. It was as if the group had vanished into thin air.

"They been taking lessons from Houdini?" Jake asked Peter, totally mystified.

"Houdini didn't disappear. He escaped from trunks and coffins and handcuffs," came the sharp retort.

Jake took one last look, then shrugged. "So much for figuring out good trails by watching them. Let's get back to work."

They rode back up the hill, returned to the grove, and spent the next few hours building two head-high dirt piles. Then, using the backs of their shovels, they patted and stomped until a firm, narrow runway ran up to the top of the first and down the far side of the last. They sat down and tore into some sandwiches, then drained their juice boxes.

"The gap's around fifteen, maybe sixteen feet," Jake said with satisfaction, stowing his shovel back in his pack. "Perfect."

Peter frowned as he stood, leaned on his shovel, and surveyed the chasm between the dirt piles. "Perfect for you, maybe. I say too wide. Doubles gaps at races are never more than fourteen feet. You just want to see me case, don't you?" He was grinning his usual Peter grin, but Jake noticed the way he kept twisting the shovel's handle in his palms.

"You'll be fine," Jake assured Peter as he stood up and brushed sandwich crumbs from his shirt. "You've done motocross freestyle; how could this be scary after that?"

"But I was into vertical air and fun tricks, not setting records for distance, like you. There's pole vaulting and then there's the long jump. Know what I mean?"

"Hey, gotta push yourself a little. It'll be fine." Jake hopped on his bike, then paused. "Just wish there weren't so many stones in this dirt."

"Rocks, Jake, are what mines are all about. And we are riding on top of a mine."

Of course, Jake thought, as he did some warm-up pedaling around the jumps, then cranked his way up the first hill. He was aware of the sound of grasshoppers and birds, and the smell of freshly turned dirt. He felt his heartbeat pick up as he pressed his shoes to the pedals and let rip. Jake liked the challenge of getting up the speed required for a wide gap. Jake could do tricks, for sure. No-footers, no-handers, and bar-twists. Lots of kids could do those. Just a matter of getting enough air, being gutsy, and practicing, practicing, practicing.

But everyone said Jake could jump farther than anyone else. Farther than racers like Peter were comfortable with. Far enough to have had a BMX sports video photographer invite him to do some extreme gaps on camera a few months back. Jake was always well aware of whatever risk he was taking, of course, and he always wore a full-face helmet and armor—all the pads needed. This is me, Jake thought as he crested and launched. This is what I like to do.

His back tire touched down on the peak of the far mound; his front tire eased down a split-second later. He lifted a fist in the air and shouted "Yes!" before rolling down the rock-studded down-ramp at high speed.

He never went for more height than he needed. He preferred to think of himself as a speeding bullet. Straight across. It had been a long, long time since he'd misjudged, cased a tire, and soared over the handlebars.

"Nice form! You did it," Peter congratulated him. "Guess I have to try it, huh?" Jake saw Peter gazing at the steep insides of the dirt piles, the place he'd end up if he jumped short. Poor Peter. He really did look nervous, Jake thought.

Peter took a few minutes, apparently psyching himself up. Then, like the racer he was, he rocketed up the first slope. His bike took to the sky with its pilot leaning low over the handlebars as if fighting an urge to grab too much air. His back tire slithered and bounced on impact, but Peter's finely tuned instincts had him leaning just right to compensate. Although his bike tottered a little on the way down, his arm was pumping the air like he'd just won an X Games purse.

"You were awesome, Peter! Told you!"

"Thanks," Peter said with a broad grin.

They each had a few more goes, Jake sprinting to Peter's sprawled body the only time he spilled. Luckily, he was fine.

"Phew! Too close," Peter said as he leaped up and inspected his bike. "Looking forward to getting on the racetrack tomorrow afternoon?"

"I guess. Why do you think that girl is going to let us on? Seems to me that'll get her in trouble with the other locals."

"I'd guess she wants something from us, but we'll just have to wait to find out what it is. Hey, do a no-footer, Jake. Can you?"

"Sure." Jake pedaled hard up the first ramp. As his bike shot into the air, he lifted his left foot off its pedal and started to arch his neck. That's when he saw what he couldn't possibly be seeing: three black-masked BMX riders emerging from a solid wall of stone.

"What the—?" he muttered, only to realize, too late, that he hadn't completed his trick and was heading for a face plant. He shed the bike so he could jump clear of it, but the far side of the second mound was determined to get a full body imprint. If only a rock embedded in it wasn't aiming for his face!

"Aiyeee," he shrieked as his face hit it hard and pain shot through his nose.

"Are you alright? Are you hurt?" Peter was shouting as he ran up the slope to his fallen buddy.

"My nose!" Jake replied, lifting his head and cupping a hand under his nose to collect the flow of blood.

Below him, three BMXers appeared near the bottom of the mound—pulled up and staring at him with amusement. Jake figured he must've been imagining the masks a minute ago, and he'd certainly been imagining the wall of rock. He watched as Micah drew closer.

"Gnarly spill," Micah said. "And nice dirt jumps.

But you're trespassing." His two companions just looked on without saying a word. Kasey seemed to be working at not meeting Jake's or Peter's eyes. Couldn't they see Jake was hurt? Didn't they care?

"This part isn't private property and you know it," Peter addressed Micah, squaring his shoulders. He moved over to Jake and pushed his hand gently under Jake's neck as if to make sure his head was tilted back far enough. "And Jake's hurt, as if you can't tell that. So get lost if you don't want to help."

"It's just the nose. I think I've broken it," Jake told Peter, the words coming out with a nasally tone as he tried to ignore the sharp pain in the middle of his face. He tilted his head back further. He pulled some tissues from his pocket and stuffed them up his nostrils. The bridge of his nose was throbbing as if a giant hammer was pounding on it. But he figured he was all right everywhere else.

"Suit yourself," Micah said, turning his bike partway around but pausing to look back. "You racing Saturday?" he asked.

"Yes," Peter replied, getting to his feet.

"Kasey here says you want to practice on our track."

"It's not … I mean, yes," Peter said, hands jammed in his shorts pockets, eyes flicking over Kasey, and waiting.

Jake saw Kasey squirming like she was on trial for

a serious crime. Since Jake hadn't decided whether to bother racing on Saturday, he kept quiet.

"No problem now that you've built us some jumps," Micah replied, mouth widening above that evil-looking purple chin scar that Jake guessed was road rash. Jake didn't like the sound of "built us some jumps." He wondered if Micah's group would ride or trash the jumps.

"But ..." Peter started, then stopped.

Micah jerked his head at Russell and Kasey as if he was the boss and they always followed his orders. They whirled their bikes around and took off, pausing just long enough for Micah to take the lead. Only Kasey looked back quickly, her face a mixture of embarrassment and apology.

5   Practice

J ake felt fine the next day. His nose was very tender if he touched it, but it had long since stopped bleeding. Despite his protests, Peter's mom had insisted on taking him to the doctor's office in Copperton. The doctor had confirmed what Jake suspected, that the nose was broken and would heal itself, and there was nothing to do except not bump it again in the near future.

So they'd returned to the cabin, and Jake had kind of enjoyed being fussed over a little. That was yesterday. Today he was bored.

"So we're supposed to meet Kasey at two o'clock at the track," Peter reminded him. "You up for that?"

"Of course," Jake replied, sitting up from where he'd been lying on the sofa. "I think I'm even good for some laps, if I'm careful not to land on my face again."

"We're outta here, then." Peter fetched his racing

bike out of the garage. He'd been busy all morning greasing the bottom bracket and cleaning his cassette hubs like his bike was a purebred show dog vying for a blue ribbon.

At the track, Jake was a little surprised to see Micah, Russell, and half a dozen other locals as well as Kasey. Then again, Kasey hadn't said she'd be on her own. She'd just said she'd make sure the kids let them on the track. Interesting that she had that kind of power when Micah seemed to be the leader. Jake guessed she'd used her role as the hardware store owner's daughter to over-rule Micah and Russell. Did she think they wouldn't hang with her if she didn't arrange store discounts for them? And why was she letting Jake and Peter on, and why did she act one way when Micah and Russell weren't around, and another way when they were? Jake didn't trust her, didn't like her.

He was certain she'd seen them when they first pulled up, but she took her time coming over. The racers they hadn't seen before glared at them initially. But after Micah said something to them, they—like Micah and Russell—studiously ignored the newcomers.

"Micah doesn't like me talking to you guys, but he won't chase you off," Kasey said when she finally did bike over. "Not today, anyway."

"We really appreciate that," Peter said enthusiastically.

"Sure." She smiled nervously at Peter. "And I was

wondering, Peter, if maybe you'd coach me a little? I mean, just keep half an eye on my riding and tell me what I need to work on?"

"No problem," Peter said with a meaningful glance at Jake.

So, that was what this was all about, thought Jake. Did it mean the other boys wouldn't do that for her? Or she didn't think they were good enough to coach? And Jake was being allowed on as Peter's friend, Peter being such a celebrity in Kasey's mind. Oh well, Jake mused as he watched Micah ride to a point nearby and pretend not to be eavesdropping.

"So here are the track rules," Kasey continued in an overly official voice. "Don't perch on the berms. Don't ride down the backsides of the jumps, 'cause they're soft and you'll wreck them. And the newbies have to run the gate for the first hour."

She paused and looked at Jake. "Your nose okay?"

"It's fine," he said.

She looked at his bike and scrunched up her face with distaste. "You don't have a racing bike? Or you're not going to do a practice today?"

Jake hung his head. She didn't have to say it like that. "This is the only bike I've got."

"Where's your bike?" Peter asked her while inching his own forward as if hoping it would catch her eye.

Just then a torrent of curses came from the bottom

of the start hill, where Russell had gone down during a practice heat. Jake watched him rise and kick his bike as his buddies tore around the first corner. Even from across the track, Jake could tell he'd snapped his chain. Jake watched the short, wiry boy in his army fatigues pull his bike off the track, let it fall beside him, yank his helmet off, and sit down in the dirt with his shaved head in his arms.

Jake hopped on his own bike and rode over. "Need a chain?" he asked Russell, who jerked his head up in surprise.

Russell studied Jake for a second, let his eyes roam to Jake's backpack. Then he lowered his head and stared at the dirt in front of him. "It's okay," he said.

Jake was silent for a moment, thinking. He guessed that Russell didn't have a chain breaker either. Jake shrugged out of his pack, pulled a chain and the tool from it, and walked over to Russell's bike.

"I could fix it," he said.

"You could, eh?" he said sarcastically. "Are you a bike mechanic or something?"

Jake smiled. "Actually, I am. Been fiddling with them for as long as I can remember. My dad taught me. He's an airplane mechanic. Or was."

"Air Force?" Russell asked, his hardened expression taking on a hint of interest as Jake began to replace the sheared-off bolts with his own spare titanium ones.

Jake glanced at the boy in his army fatigues. "Nope. Is yours?"

"Army," he said, lifting his head proudly, maybe even defiantly, Jake thought.

Jake finished fixing the chain and stepped back to wipe his hands on his trousers. "So what happens now with the army base shutting down?" he ventured.

Anger flashed across the boy's face. "We have to move when my dad gets back from the Middle East." He turned to look at the racers on the track. Jake noticed that Micah, Kasey, and Peter were setting themselves up at the start gate. Micah was paused there, giving Russell a mean look.

"How much for the chain?" Russell asked like he was suddenly in a big hurry to go.

"I got it for thirty bucks," Jake said. "Okay to pay me back tomorrow. I trust you. See you on the track."

"Thanks." Russell hesitated. "I'm Russell Allen, by the way. You racing on that?"

"I'm Jake Evans, and it's my only bike," Jake muttered.

Russell peered at him, eyebrows arched in amazement. He was silent for a moment, then lifted his arm to jab a finger at a locked shed beside the track. "There's a demo racing bike in there. Kasey's dad's. Ask Kasey. Thanks again," he added as he biked away fast. Jake coughed in the cloud of dust he raised.

Jake didn't feel like asking the weird redhead for any favors, so he entered the track on his jump bike, attracting a few stares from the racers. Only one other person, a little kid, had a jump bike on the course.

For the next hour, Jake, Peter, and the locals rode hard on the track—high-lowing the corners, rubbing tires, banging elbows, and challenging each other to games of foot-down.

"Remember, whoever puts their foot down is out. Last one riding is the winner," Kasey called out to the little kids in an unnecessarily bossy tone, Jake thought.

Jake's bike made him hopelessly slow, but since his broken nose started throbbing when he got up any speed anyway, he didn't really care. He probably shouldn't have even tried coming on the track with this bike, but it was better than watching from the sidelines.

It was a strange workout, considering hardly any of the kids said a word to the two, not even Kasey after her initial briefing. They just seemed to tolerate Jake and Peter's presence as everyone lined up, eight across, for the start gate heats.

Any time Jake tried to start a conversation, he was given the cold shoulder, even by Russell. Peter, he noticed, didn't even try, except with Kasey. And she responded with measured, almost reluctant politeness when he offered a riding tip or two. Certainly, she offered none of the gushy respect or open friendliness she'd exhibited in the store just after she'd heard Peter's last name. What a two-faced girl. What was with this locals-versus-weekenders thing, anyway? On whose orders were the kids not speaking to them? Had to be Micah, he guessed.

"Riders ready. Watch the lights," a parent helper called out.

Seconds later, they were off. The parent's commentary over the megaphone got more and more excitable.

"Micah has the holeshot coming out of the gate, but Braden goes low into the corner. Oh! Chase has been forced up on the berm. Russell pre-manuals the first bump in the rhythm section. Way to go! Kasey completes the whole third straight on her back wheel. Lucas jumps the triple, but Will manuals and squeezes past while Lucas is in the air. Now they're banging elbows in the second corner ..."

Peter looked a little rusty to Jake, but was improving with every lap. Micah was way out ahead of anyone else, Russell lapping at his heels.

Jake heard Micah coach Russell numerous times, even though it looked to Jake like Russell knew all the moves that Micah was advising him on. But maybe Jake was wrong about that, because Russell seemed to hunger for Micah's attention. Kasey, on the other hand, appeared to be having a bad day. She was pretty good on the rhythm section, but cased her tire every time on the triple, and seemed a little slow through the corners.

"I'm not doing the berms right," she complained at one point while standing near Micah as Peter was taking a break.

Micah didn't respond. In fact, not once that afternoon did Jake hear him offer Kasey any advice. She obviously needed it. She was good, but not great. No wonder she'd bargained for Peter's help. So why was Micah helping Russell but not Kasey? Because she'd let weekenders onto the track? Because she was too new in town to be a real local by Micah's standards? Then again, why should Jake care?

"Last gate," Micah called out late in the afternoon. Then, to Jake's surprise, he turned to Kasey and said, "How about you get that spare racing bike out for Jake?"

Jake was surprised. It wasn't Micah's bike; it was Kasey's dad's. So what did Micah have to do with it? Jake would've asked Kasey for the bike earlier, but he'd been too proud. Clearly, Russell had suggested it to Micah or Kasey as a way of thanking Jake for the bike repair help. So Micah wasn't such a bad guy, even if he'd waited till the end of the session. Jake looked at Russell, who was carefully looking in the other direction, as if he didn't want to take credit for the favor in Micah's sight.

"Can't," Kasey was saying. "Haven't got the key to the shed and Dad's out of town."

Micah looked surprised, then shrugged his shoulders and tossed an apologetic look to Jake. "Too bad." That's when Peter spoke up.

"Need that shed open?" he addressed Kasey. "I could do that for you."

Kasey squinted her eyes at him, and Micah and Russell turned their heads toward Peter.

"I said I don't have the key," Kasey said.

"And I said that's no problem, if you're okay with Jake trying the spare racing bike," Peter replied. "I know how to pick a lock without hurting the lock. Are you okay with me showing you that?"

Kasey sat back on her bike seat, raised her hands to her hips, and arranged her mouth in a pout. "Dad said I could use the bike whenever I wanted, or loan it to people if I think they'll be careful. So if I had the key, it'd be okay to open it." She hesitated. "You can open it without hurting the lock?"

Peter smiled and nodded importantly.

"Let's see you," she said.

Peter strode over to the shed. He pulled something out of his pants pocket and bent over the lock. Three seconds and he had it open. No damage to the lock. Jake knew it was three seconds because he was counting under his breath. Peter made him do that every night while he tried to shave time off his lock-picking exercises. Of course, it's one thing to practice for a magic show back at the cabin, and a whole different thing to do it for real in front of a bunch of semi-hostile locals. What was Peter thinking?

Jake did a quick scan of the faces. Micah had crossed his arms but was trying to hide a smile as he snuck a glance at Kasey. Russell was scratching his head. Kasey's mouth was frozen open. Peter seemed to interpret the silence as permission to wheel the bike out of the shed and neatly relock the shed door.

"So Jake can borrow the bike?" Peter asked.

"Sure," Kasey said, removing her helmet to run a hand through her hair and shaking her head like she was still trying to figure out how Peter had done that.

Jake knew what he should do next. He looked Micah in the eyes and said, "Thanks." Then he turned quickly to Kasey and said, "It's a great looking bike. I'll be real careful on this practice run."

"You'd better," Kasey warned, trying too hard to look stern, Jake thought.

Then Jake nodded to Russell, who gave him the slightest nod back.

"Gate's waiting!" Micah called out, and everyone hurried to get on the gate.

6   Oxygen

"**E**ven if we get the asking price for this place tomorrow, Laura, I think we have to switch Peter back to public school. We need to tighten up on our spending much more than we are."

Peter froze and felt his chest go rigid. His breath felt choked out of him. He'd arrived just outside the cabin well ahead of Jake, and obviously too quietly for his parents to have heard his bike tires on the dirt path. His dad's voice sounded miserable. The living room window was open in the afternoon heat and they surely hadn't meant him to hear that.

"Honey, one of us is bound to get called back to work soon. Please don't talk like that," he heard his mother reply in a tight voice.

"Says who? You read the papers, sweetie. You know it's getting worse, not better. Maybe we should sell our house in Seattle and move here. I could get my real estate license or something."

Real estate license? But you're an airplane pilot! Peter felt his throat tighten up. He glanced back, saw Jake approaching, knew he had to make some noise. Maybe in a few more seconds.

"Richard, really. Listen what a few beers this afternoon have done to you. We need to keep our chins up for Peter's sake. And you need to get out of this cabin somewhere other than to Copperton Saloon. Maybe do a family outing. Spend some time with Peter."

Jake rolled up on his jump bike, the borrowed demo back in the shed. "Good workout, huh?" He was studying Peter's face.

"Great workout," Peter agreed, a little louder than usual. "And your nose didn't hurt?"

Jake shrugged and smiled. "Just like the doctor said. It'll mend itself in a couple of weeks."

"You always did get your nose out of joint too easily."

"Very funny."

"Jake, Peter! How was the racetrack? Nice of those Copperton kids to let you practice with them." His mom was striding out the door with her overly friendly flight-attendant voice and fluttery hands. His dad shuffled to the door frame behind her, forcing a smile.

"Hello, son. Hi, Jake. No more nose jobs today, I hope."

"Nope."

"We were just saying, Peter, that we need some fresh air," Peter's mother said. "I hear there's a corn maze not far from town. How about the four of us do a little outing there this evening?"

Peter winked at Jake. "Sorry, Mom, sounds a little lame. You and Dad should go, though. Jake and I were thinking it'd be fun to sleep in the pup tent tonight. Okay with you if we hike up over the hills and camp out?"

He tried not to feel guilty when his mom's face fell.

"Well, your father and I could take the bigger tent and we could have a family campout. We could build a campfire and have a marshmallow roast! Would you like that, Richard? It'd take your mind off things."

Things, Peter thought bitterly.

"Whatever you all decide," Peter's dad responded, sounding tired.

How could he be tired, Peter wondered? He just puttered around the cabin all day, then visited the bar in the afternoons—which usually prompted a scolding from Peter's mother. Peter couldn't remember his dad ever going to a bar before he'd gotten laid off work. But maybe he had between flights with the other pilots. Maybe it was no big deal. Still, Peter didn't like it any more than his mother did. And didn't like how his parents had been arguing more and more, sometimes within earshot of Jake.

"Okay with me," Jake was saying politely.

Peter tossed his buddy a look. "That'd be real fun another time," he interjected, giving his mother an encouraging smile. "But I was thinking just Jake and me. Okay with you for one night?"

"Okay," his mom said, twisting her hands a little. "I just thought the maze would be fun."

"A maze," Peter's dad reflected, staring into the dark blue of the lake. "Remember when we used to get Peter those little books of puzzle mazes?" He chuckled loudly.

"Dad, that's when I was like five," Peter protested, but his father didn't seem to register his reply.

"The last time I did one of those pencil mazes was at 25,000 feet with no oxygen," Richard told the group while staring at the lake.

"Huh?" Peter said, wondering how many beers his dad had had.

"It was part of flight training. We were in this pressurized training chamber—not really in the air—and had to turn off our regulators, take off our oxygen masks, and do puzzle mazes."

"No way! How long could you last like that?" Jake asked.

"The whole idea was to see how long we could last

before we got hypoxia—oxygen deprivation."

"And?" Peter tried to hurry up the story while picturing his heroes, Houdini and Blaine, winning the exercise hands-down.

"Well, as I was finishing the maze, I got hot and cold flashes and tingling in my hands and feet. Some of the pilots even threw up."

"Gee, thanks for telling us that, Dad."

"Hypoxia lowers your night vision, too," his dad said. "And once you start getting it, you have only a few seconds to react."

"That's why flight attendants tell parents to put their own oxygen masks on before taking care of their children," Laura inserted with a smile.

"Right," Peter remarked, rolling his eyes.

"All right, boys," Laura Montpetit said. "I'll help you find the camping gear, and then Dad and I will do the corn maze. Unless you want to change your minds. Oh, I forgot to ask. How were your practice runs? Ready for that race Saturday?"

"I think I need more practice," Peter replied. "Those Copperton kids aren't bad."

Now there's an understatement, Jake thought. Micah was at least as good as Peter, and Russell was pretty fast, too.

"They must spend lots of time on that course. That's about all there is to do in this town," Peter added.

"Well, with no mine or army base here any more, I don't suppose the community can afford facilities for their children. We're very lucky, I suppose," his mom mused.

"And they're lucky to have us weekenders for the money we spend in town," Peter added, ignoring his father's frown.

"I don't think you'd talk like that if the shoe were on the other foot," said Richard Montpetit.

A few hours later, laden with heavy backpacks, Peter and Jake pedaled up the hill, choosing a site against a long rock wall not far from their dirt jumps. After they'd roasted wieners on sticks and eaten baked beans out of a can, they put their campfire out and looked up at the stars. Frogs croaked and crickets chirped in uncertain harmony.

Peter watched the full moon rise. He liked all the little shadows across its sphere. The light from the moon illuminated the funny little hillocks, which looked like the work of giant moles. It cast an eerie glow on the abandoned mine buildings and reflected a ghostly white off the long rock wall that ran down from their campsite.

Peter sat up. "Fireflies," he observed.

"Nah, bike lights," Jake responded.

Peter continued to sit very still, listening. He was amazed to hear the distant crunch of bike tires on gravel, and see the dots of light grow larger. He counted the pinpricks of bouncing light: three. Closer and closer they grew, heading toward a lower section of the wall against which the boys had pitched their tent. Now he could see them silhouetted in the moonlight, three ETs—extraterrestrials—biking against the moon. They seemed to be heading for a point not twenty yards below the boys.

"They're going to hit the rock wall," Peter whispered, shaking his head. But to his astonishment, they disappeared. And the night returned to its frog and cricket throb.

7 Tunnels

Jake scrambled to his feet and moved toward the wall. Ghosts don't ride bikes, do they?

"I'll grab the flashlight from the tent," Peter declared. "Must be an opening in the wall."

An opening, Jake thought, of course. But where? And why? And who?

They stumbled through the moonlit terrain, their only flashlight's tiny beam trained on the wall. The search would have been useless without the full moon. What chance did two D batteries have against dark rock at night?

"Found it," Jake marveled, running his hand along an opening chipped into a wall of concrete blocks. "Someone's taken a sledgehammer to this bit. It's like a little doorway knocked out of a bigger, bricked-up opening."

He peered through the hole into what looked like

a dark tunnel beyond. The opening was large enough to admit a kid ducked down on a bike. But why would anyone—

"Hello in there!" Peter was saying, his head stuck into the opening.

"Hello in there," came a faint echo.

"It's an old mining tunnel," Peter said, as if Jake couldn't figure that out. Peter turned his head sideways and touched a finger to his cheek. "There's air circulating through it. Maybe that means there's an opening somewhere else?"

"Insane," Jake said, sticking his head in, too. "It's deadly dark and it smells musty. Biking here would be dangerous, even with headlights on. No way a bike light would let you see where the heck you're going." He grabbed Peter's flashlight and shone it on the walls, ceiling, and floor. Water droplets winked at him. The smell of wet dirt and stone made him think about caving he'd done. The faintest flow of air tickled his face.

"Hello," he couldn't help calling out. Sure enough, a faint echo called back.

He jumped as he felt a hand on his shoulder, but it was only Peter pushing around him to get inside. Peter grabbed the flashlight out of Jake's hands.

"Peter Montpetit, don't you even think about going in there," Jake commanded, a flash of panic engulfing him.

"Why not?" Peter was shining his flashlight in a big arc. "Hey, the floor and walls are totally smooth. And the ceiling's not so low once you get in here. But it's dark, dark, dark. No one could bike in here. Except that they are. We weren't imagining that, were we?"

Jake leaned a little farther into the entrance and listened carefully. There was no sound but the dripping of water and Peter's breathing. "I don't think so, but I can't hear anything. Maybe they have wall switches for ceiling lights farther in," he joked. "But I'm not coming in, and you're not going any farther. You don't know if there are poisonous gases, you don't know if you can breathe in there, you don't know if it might collapse, and you don't know if some wild animal hangs out farther in." The last bit was lame, but Jake didn't want Peter doing something stupid.

"You can't stop me without coming in here yourself," Peter taunted as he moved a few steps further. "Anyway, three people are in here somewhere. Why should they have all the fun?"

"Peter, please." Jake's hand tightened on the cold archway of the chipped-out entry.

"Just a couple more yards," Peter's echoing voice promised. "If there are any wild animals, they've already eaten Copperton's BMX team. So they wouldn't still be hungry."

"We don't know it's Micah and friends," Jake said.

"Hah, as if we don't!" came a voice getting slightly fainter.

Jake sighed and shuffled ahead a few steps into the inky darkness. The tunnel's floor was surprisingly level, even if was just blasted, exposed rock. Judging by what he could see from Peter's bobbing flashlight, the rails had long since been torn out except for the occasional piece lying haphazardly in the corridor. The walls and ceiling had been sprayed with something like stucco. A kind of roughened concrete, like in the fake-stone animal dens at the zoo. Shotcrete, the word came to him. "Okay, if a rock falls on your head, I'm here to pull you out. But you're being stupid."

"How about brave and adventurous?" Peter teased, pausing for Jake to catch up. He shone the flashlight on the floor beneath his feet. "None of that sprayed concrete on the floor. It's kind of rough, but not too bad to ride on. Hey, the tunnel splits here."

Jake, shivering in the dampness of the head-high space, watched Peter's flashlight flick left, right, left, right. The corridor on the left headed steeply up. The one on the right stayed level.

"You said only a few yards. You promised."

"But that was before I knew the tunnel had a fork in it. Hmmm, which way do you think they went?"

"I don't care and I'm not going one step farther."

A higher-pitched echo mocked him: "I don't care

and I'm not going one step farther." Jake shivered again and took a step backwards.

"Pick a number between ten and twenty, old buddy," Peter urged Jake.

"Fifteen," Jake said impatiently.

"Right then. I'm walking fifteen paces up that steep ramp, absolutely no farther. Then we'll go back to our tent. Promise."

Jake sighed and wrapped his arms around himself. "Go then, you idiot."

Jake counted the sounds of Peter's shoes crunching as he watched their only light disappear. He'd counted thirteen foot treads, unsure of whether he'd missed one or two, when he heard someone mumble, "Need to sit down."

"Peter?" he called out. No answer. "Peter? Peter?"

Jake's shrieks were echoing as he worked his way toward Peter. His fingers touched the damp smoothness of the shotcrete-sprayed walls. He had taken about ten steps past the fork when he started to feel lightheaded. He gulped deeply and held his breath in case some kind of noxious gases were around. He took another two steps forward, his shoes moving cautiously up the steep incline, when he came to Peter's slumped figure. The flashlight, still shining, was in Peter's limp hand. He looked like he'd sat down, then fallen asleep.

Refusing to release his breath, Jake bent forward, grabbed the flashlight, then grasped Peter under his armpits. He dragged him down the ramp—down, down, down, fighting his need to open his mouth and take a breath. Peter's slumped figure was heavy, but Jake had never moved so fast in his life. When he reached the fork, he gulped air and dropped to his knees on the cold, hard floor. Heart racing, he put his ear over Peter's open mouth.

"You're breathing, Peter. You're still breathing," he said, fighting back tears. He shook Peter gently by the shoulders and shone the flashlight on his face. That's when he heard a strange whirring sound, like a ghost train moving toward him. Instinctively, he put his arms around his head and leaned across Peter to protect him. A shout and the alarming sound of brakes screeching rang in his head.

"What the devil—?" Micah's voice sounded immediately behind him.

Then everything seemed to happen at once. Bikes clattering to the floor, feet running toward him. The jolt of Micah shoving him aside and sliding an arm under Peter's neck. The sound of Peter moaning. And the faint outline of Micah's frightening face in the glow of Peter's flashlight.

Micah looked like a space alien with bugged-out eyes. He seemed to have a miniature pair of black binoculars strapped around his helmeted head. Jake turned as two more bodies leaned over him. Backlit by the headlights of three fallen bikes, they were Russell and Kasey wearing the same black binoculars.

"Jake?" Peter was saying as he seemed to sway where he was sitting. "I felt dizzy, so I sat down, and then I think I fainted. I'm okay now."

"No, it's Micah," the figure crouched over him responded. "What are you doing here? What happened? Jake, how long was he blacked out?"

"One minute max," Jake responded.

Micah grabbed the flashlight from Jake and shone it on his gloved right hand. "How many fingers am I holding up, Peter?"

Jake saw Peter staring at Micah's face. "Night-vision goggles?" he asked groggily. "Micah?"

"How many fingers, Peter?" Micah repeated, whipping off his goggles with his other arm. Even in the dim light, Jake could see that Micah's face was coated in dirt and sweat, except for where the goggles had been. He'd transformed from an alien to a raccoon.

"Two," Peter replied correctly, looking from Micah to Jake. "Jake, you okay?"

"I'm okay," Jake said, relief flooding him. "And you're okay?"

Micah slid his arm out from under Peter's head

and turned to Jake. His face went from concerned to accusing.

"We saw you bike in here," Jake began, "and Peter followed you. He went up that left tunnel and collapsed. I dragged him out while holding my breath. Was it poisonous gases? Is he going to be okay?"

Micah continued glaring at Jake. "He's very, very lucky you were behind him but not too close behind. You're both nuts to be in here; you don't know anything about these tunnels."

"And you're not nuts to be in here?" Peter spoke up, apparently having recovered his breath. "If there are poisonous gases, I mean."

Micah turned his hardened gaze back to Peter. "This is a hardrock mine. There are no poisonous gases. That's mostly in soft rock mines, like coal or salt. But there are pockets of oxygen-deficient atmosphere here," he continued.

Oxygen-deficient atmosphere? Jake thought. And Peter calls these guys hicks. Hicks don't talk like that. And hicks don't have night-vision goggles, which he knew cost several hundred dollars each. And these guys are using them to ride through mining tunnels where people can collapse for lack of air? He shook his head. He'd wake up any moment in his bed back at Peter's cabin, right?

"So Peter ran out of oxygen and collapsed?" Jake asked.

"If he went up that ramp, yes," Micah replied. "That's a bad spot."

"You need an oxygen meter, like Micah has," Kasey inserted.

Jake turned the flashlight on Kasey's face. Strands of her frizzy hair stuck to her face beside the helmet. The black night-vision goggles looked very odd against her freckled face. Jake turned to watch Micah pull something off his belt that looked like a pocket calculator with a little light on it.

"Twenty-one percent oxygen where we're standing right now," he ruled. "That's the perfect amount. But if I walk up that tunnel"—he pointed to the one down which Jake had dragged Peter—"this would beep within a couple of steps to warn me. That tunnel's no good." He replaced the oxygen meter in its holster on his belt. "Without one of these, and especially if you don't know the routes in here, you can die. You got lucky, Peter," he finished, rising. "Now get out of here, don't ever come back in, and stop following us. And if you say a word to anyone about us biking in here, you'll be way worse than sorry."

Jake looked at Russell, who hadn't said a word.

"He means that," Russell said, as if on cue.

"Understood," Jake replied. He was still feeling a

little overwhelmed by Peter's close call, and he felt grateful for Micah's concern and knowledge. So he couldn't really blame anyone in the group for being stern with them.

The three BMXers retrieved their bikes, adjusted their goggles, and stood on their pedals.

"Wait a minute," Peter was saying. "Where'd you get night-vision goggles and oxygen meters? And hasn't anyone noticed you putting holes in these tunnel plugs?"

Micah sat back down on his bike seat, his black goggle eyes directed Peter's way. He said nothing for a very long moment, then rested an elbow on his handlebars.

"The army donated the goggles to us," he said, but a chuckle from Kasey exposed his lie.

"I found a box of them at the dump," Russell piped up, pride in his voice. "Nice of the army to leave something in Copperton."

"And Micah borrows the oxygen meter from his dad," Kasey revealed. The smile that came over Micah's face made Jake wonder whether Micah's dad knew about the loan of the meter. Not likely, he thought. "His dad used to be the mine manager here."

"My dad and grandpa both mined here," Micah said, drawing himself up. "I'd be doing the same if the stupid owners hadn't shut it down." The bitterness in his voice was enough to silence the little crowd in the tunnel.

"And the plugs?" Peter pushed.

"There's dozens of entrances and exits to the mining tunnels," Russell spoke up. "Most of them are stopped up with concrete blocks. A few of the older ones have timber bulkheads. This one had a few blocks fallen out already, so it wasn't so hard to widen." He smiled at his companions. "No one has noticed so far."

"We'll blame it on you if they ever do," Micah finished darkly. "Now get out of here. That's an order."

8   Fathers and Sons

The flame of Peter's candle blew left, flickered a pretty blue as it struggled against the draft, then went out.

"Mom," Peter complained as his mother stepped into the cabin with arms full of grocery bags. "You let the door slam and my candle went out."

"And why would you need a candle lit at ten in the morning on a bright, sunny day? Oh, of course. A new magic trick?" She beamed at him and set her bags down on the table.

"Yup, a good one. Hey, is Dad coming to watch the race this afternoon?"

Peter watched his mother frown and check her watch. "Maybe if you go fetch him," she said wearily.

Peter noticed the dark circles under his mom's eyes. She didn't have to say where to fetch his dad from. The increasing amount of time Richard

Montpetit was spending in the local bar was never spoken of between mother and son. Peter felt an ache in his chest. He wanted his dad to come to the race. But he didn't want to "fetch him," because someone might see him.

"Do I have to?"

"Yes, Peter, please. Where's Jake?"

"He went early to help set up."

"Okay. You get your father home for lunch, then go on down there, and we'll show up before the race starts, okay? We're proud of you, Peter."

"Thanks," Peter said but knew it had come out like a sigh.

He grabbed his street bike and did a half-hearted catwalk on the way to the Copperton Saloon. With his eyes downcast and heart heavy, he didn't even notice someone approaching the bar on a bike from the opposite direction. When he raised his head from locking his bike up, he froze.

"Micah."

"Peter," Micah replied evenly while locking his bike up.

The two stared at each other for a moment, as if reluctant to carry out whatever task they were in this part of town for. Peter certainly didn't want Micah seeing him going into the bar to fetch his father. His father was more respectable than how that looked. He wasn't a bum who drank at this time of day. At least, he wouldn't be once he got working again. But Micah was just standing there. Was he headed into the bar, too?

The standoff was starting to feel awkward. Someone had to either start up a conversation or move. So Peter nodded to Micah ever so slightly and walked into the bar on what felt like spongy feet. He drew in his breath when he realized Micah was two steps behind him.

What a dark, dingy place. It reeked of spilled alcohol, and the smoke made his eyes sting. Why would anyone want to spend a sunny summer day here when they had a cabin on a sparkling lake? Peter spotted his father sitting alone in a booth, a beer in front of him. His shoulders were hunched and his eyes were studying the table glumly. Peter didn't mean to turn his head, but there was Micah, standing right beside him, staring at a weathered-looking man in a booth one over from Richard. The man's eyes were on a hockey game on the television affixed to the wall across the room. He was cheering, then jeering the action with bright eyes and a dancing fist. But his eyes really lit up when he spotted Micah.

"Son, come on over. Guess who's winning? Oh, and you're with a friend. Bring him here so I can meet him."

Peter felt his face flush bright pink. When he

dared a glance at Micah, he saw his face was the same color. But before either could say anything, Richard looked up.

"Peter!" he said, his eyes darting left and right as if checking to see who else had seen him in here. "I was just about to come home."

Yeah right, Peter thought, looking at his father's full glass. Peter stepped forward.

"This your boy?" Micah's dad asked Richard, as if noticing him for the first time. "Come join us." He patted the worn vinyl covering of the booth seat beside him. Peter hung his head as his father rose unsteadily and steered himself to Micah's father's booth. The vinyl squeaked as he sat down a little too hard, beer glass held high.

"I'm Sven," Micah's dad was saying as he held his hand out to Richard. "Sven Rubenson. And this is my son Micah."

Peter's father set his beer down. The boys remained standing hesitantly near the booth. "Hi, Sven. I'm Richard Montpetit, unemployed pilot. Thinking of moving to scenic Copperton. Beautiful town you have here."

Peter wanted to sink right through the stained floorboards as Micah surveyed Peter's dad, then swung his eyes to Peter. For a moment, Micah's and Peter's eyes met. Peter felt a flicker of empathy pass between them. Both were here to fetch their dads, and both were humiliated about it.

Peter watched his father pump Sven's hand a few too many times. "My boy's Peter," Richard continued, waving vaguely at Peter. "Didn't know he knew your son, but he's a real outgoing kid. Sit down boys, tell us something new."

"Mom says come home for lunch," Peter said lamely, lowering himself into the seat as if it was an electric chair. "So you can make the race this afternoon."

"Sure, no hurry," Richard replied, beaming at Peter, Micah, and Sven.

Micah slid easily into the booth beside his dad and across from Peter, folding his big hands in his lap. His eyes lifted to the television screen. Peter got the sense he'd been here many times before.

"Hey, Micah!" the bartender called out. "You missed the penalty shot."

Micah unfolded his hands and waved casually at the bartender in response, eyes still on the game.

Sven slid an arm around Micah's shoulders, beaming with pride. Micah squared his shoulders at the touch and gave his dad an easy smile, but there was a sadness, a weariness to the way the smile faded quickly and the gaze returned to the hockey action.

"So, Peter, are you an MX racer like Micah here?"

"BMX, not MX," Micah corrected his father.

"Yes, Mr. Rubenson, I'm a BMX racer." Peter studied Sven's yellow, nicotine-stained fingers and his kind, grizzled face with its distant gaze.

Sven pushed his beer away and smiled broadly at Richard. "So you're going to watch this race too?"

"Absolutely. Wouldn't miss my son racing," Richard said, although he'd hardly looked at Peter since he'd come in the door. He clutched his beer glass. "You live here in Copperton? Reminds me of the town I grew up in. Makes me want to live in a small town again. Get back to my roots, you know?"

What? Peter thought.

"Lived here all my life," Sven replied. "Yeah, it'd be a good town if there were jobs. Used to be manager at the mine before they closed it down."

Micah raised his head at this and looked Peter in the eyes. Peter meant to smile or nod at him in return but instead found himself shifting his gaze to his own father, then dropping it to his lap.

"I'm on the dole now, like most everyone else in town," Sven continued. "But Micah here's gonna make somethin' of himself, he will. Smart boy."

Micah's dad was obviously fond and proud of his son, Peter thought. And Micah seems kind of used to him being unemployed and hanging out in the bar. Well, Peter wasn't about to get used to his dad doing the same. His dad was a pilot from Seattle. This talk about moving to Copperton was just the beer.

"Dad, come now," Peter pleaded, his hand on his dad's elbow. "Right away."

"Whoa, whoa, what's the emergency?" Richard replied. "These boys are always in a hurry, aren't they, Sven?"

"Always," Sven agreed, eyes lighting up again as he pushed his beer further away and looked at Micah.

Peter couldn't take it anymore, the shame of Micah knowing his dad was unemployed and drinking a little too much. He gripped his dad's nearest arm with both his hands, pulled him up, and steered him toward the door, with a parting, apologetic glance at Micah.

"Bye, Richard. Bye, Peter. See you soon," Sven called out, in a tone so genuinely friendly that you'd think the two families were long-time friends.

9   First Heat

"**H**ey, you're just in time," Jake said as Peter arrived at the racecourse. "We're both registered, and it's three heats and a main."

The "main" was the final event. To advance to it, a competitor had to do well in all three qualifying rounds, called heats or "motos." Only eight could race within each division in the mains. Peter was confident he'd be one of them. He wasn't sure about Jake.

The place was buzzing with excitement. Peter figured almost 200 people were milling about, so no way could they all be locals. He recognized a few kids from the lake, including some cute preschoolers excitedly sprinting around on "pit bikes," little BMXs. He wondered if any of the weekenders had ever entered a BMX race before. But what the heck, it was a big deal for a town like Copperton.

"Track looks mostly the same," said Peter. "They've just added a triple jump, hey?"

"Sure have," Jake replied.

Peter ran his eye around all 1,000 feet of track. Like most courses, it started with metal gates for eight bikes at the top of a rise. When the gates dropped, riders would go full-speed down a wide drop leading into a turn. After that, the track narrowed and began throwing a variety of challenges at competitors—bumps, hills, and curves designed to make them speed, slide, jump, and crash. Then came the finish, a roughly ten-yard straight that demanded furious pedaling just when you were about done for.

"A hundred riders?" Peter said. "And enough guys in our division to make a main event. Who'd've believed it?"

"Yup," Jake answered. "That's lots of people for Copperton, eh?"

"It's amazing." Peter started visualizing his bike's movements through each and every feature.

"Peter, what's with the sign on your family's car?" Jake asked.

"Huh?" Peter was annoyed at being distracted from his visualization exercises.

"Your BMW. There's a 'For Sale' sign on it. Why would they bother now when no one around here's going to buy it? We're going to be pretty squished going back to Seattle if all we have is their Tercel."

"Our BMW's not for sale," Peter said, still surveying the course.

"Yup. I'm afraid it is."

Peter turned to look at Jake, saw he was serious. Jake pointed to the parking lot. Peter shaded his eyes and located the sleek silver sedan. So, his parents had arrived and were somewhere around. Even from this distance, he could see some kind of sign on it. He turned and sprinted up to the lot, Jake at his heels. He stared at the sign, grinding his teeth. He pulled off his baseball cap and mopped his forehead. The day's heat was really catching up to him. A voice echoed flatly in his brain: Want to live in a small town again. Get back to my roots, you know?

"Dad," Peter pronounced, his voice sounding hollow. "He's having some kind of meltdown." Things weren't that bad, were they? His dad was just frightened, that's all. He was overreacting. And Jake was right. No one around here would buy it. Except—except people from the lake.

"Oh," Jake said uncertainly.

Peter walked up to the BMW and wriggled an arm through a gap in a partially open back window. With one grab, he ripped the "For Sale" sign off the window, then dropped it resolutely into a nearby garbage can.

"So, old buddy," he said, wiping his hands on his

jeans, "let's go get ready for our first heat. You riding the demo bike?"

"Kasey hasn't decided," Jake said, frowning.

"Well, if you do, I'd better watch my behind," Peter joked.

As they walked back down the hill from the parking lot, they spotted Kasey with a lineup of younger girls holding pieces of paper and pens and whispering through smiles to one another. Kasey stood tall and at arm's length from them, like some kind of pop star accustomed to the attention, as she scribbled her autograph.

"So," Peter said under his breath, "she really is a name racer."

"Locally, anyway," Jake replied dryly.

"Can't wait to see her race. She's definitely improved with a bit of coaching." A sideways glance at Jake made him sense that Jake didn't like Kasey. He didn't blame Jake. She was moody and a bit full of herself, though less so around Peter. He got the sense that no one liked her except maybe her loopy father and little-girl fans.

Twenty minutes later, Peter was fully dressed in a long-sleeved jersey and pants. Underneath he wore the one-piece armor that mountain bikers wear, complete with chest, elbow, and spine protection. He also wore full-fingered gloves and a full-face helmet.

Mr. Lowe from the hardware store was making a little speech from the moto shed promoting "Copperton's first annual BMX extravaganza."

"And now," he announced importantly, "my daughter Kasey Lowe will lead us in singing the national anthem."

Peter saw Jake roll his eyes, but Peter strained his ears as he stood with the rest of the crowd. Kasey's notes were right on pitch. She's good, he decided. And she has lots of potential at biking, too. He was kind of proud of being a coach.

When the music finished, Peter started some warm-up stretches while looking around. He'd been on the circuit long enough to know some of the American bikers who'd driven up for this Canadian race. And he was relieved—none of the guys he knew could beat him were here. But he didn't know the Canadians as well, which is probably why he hadn't heard of Kasey, Micah, or Russell before.

Mr. Lowe was lucky to have attracted so many bikers, Peter thought. Imagine some of them driving 300 miles to a rundown town in the middle of nowhere. Showed how the circuit needed more races. Mr. Lowe was also lucky so many weekenders had decided to give a new sport a try and rent bikes from the hardware store.

Peter spotted Micah doing warm-ups. It made the

entire Copperton Saloon scene start replaying in his head. He looked away quickly, his face burning. He still felt angry that Micah knew about his dad being unemployed, and that his dad had spouted that stuff about wanting to move to Copperton. We're not like you, Peter thought. We're from Seattle, just here on vacation. Mom and Dad will have their jobs back any day.

He stuffed his hands into his gloves, noticed they were shaking slightly. He had to win. He had to beat Micah today. He almost wished some of the big shots were here to ask for advice, though. He was unsure about some of the moves the course required.

"Feeling ready?"

Peter almost jumped out of his skin. He turned to see Kasey, fully suited up in white jersey and trousers, her helmet in one hand. As her red hair ruffled in the breeze, he figured she wasn't as bad looking as he'd first thought. And she was talking to him in that friendly tone she used when the Copperton guys weren't around.

"Yeah. How about you?"

"Very ready, thanks to you." She smiled warmly. He wished she was like this all the time, not chilly and bossy when with Micah and Russell.

"Just me? Doesn't Micah ever help you?"

She frowned. "Never. He only coaches Russell, 'cause Russell grew up here like him. Guess I'm not a real local yet for him," she said with a hint of bitterness. "But Dad and I are staying here, and there's hardly anyone else my age, so I just keep trying to fit in."

So trying to fit in meant doing whatever Micah said and being as cold to weekenders as Micah was, Peter thought. Except while being coached out of earshot of Micah. He was starting to get the picture. She was desperate enough to get better at BMX to "buy" Peter's coaching by offering him access to the track. And at the same time, she was trying to control the town boss—Micah—by wielding whatever power those hardware-store discounts were worth. Did she think no one would like her if she didn't manipulate them? She was way too desperate to fit in here in Copperton, Peter thought. And why was she so desperate to improve, anyway?

"You really like racing?" he asked her.

She sighed and hesitated. "I did at first. Now sometimes it feels like something I do for Dad. He's crazier about me winning than I am. Guess it gives him something to do since Mom died," she added with downcast eyes.

Oops, better change the subject, Peter thought.

"Hey," he said. "Any idea what line Micah's going to take on the triple jump?" She probably wouldn't know, but it would help him a lot if she did.

She looked around to make sure no one could hear

them, then leaned in to whisper, "I heard him tell Russell to double manual through both dips with his tire up. He said not to try jumping it 'cause the corner after it isn't banked enough."

A load of stress lifted from Peter's shoulders. He'd been worrying a lot about that part of the course. "Hey, thanks," he said, smiling big at her.

She returned the smile. "So, any advice for getting the holeshot?"

He'd just begun coaching her on that and one other question she had when they were interrupted.

"All riders to staging," Mr. Lowe was saying through the scratchy megaphone. "Is everyone—and I mean everyone—ready for Copperton's first annual BMX extravaganza?"

"Dad," Kasey muttered. "He's so embarrassing."

"He's just a dad," Peter said lightly. "A dad running a race to help you make friends."

Oops, wrong thing to say. Kasey's eyes narrowed and she took a step back from Peter. "Dad," she declared in an angry voice, "needs a life. He's suffocating me. I can make my own friends. He has to stop pushing me and bragging about me." She stopped suddenly, like she realized she'd said all that aloud. Her face turned rosy pink. For a second, Peter thought about reaching out to comfort her. Then she took yet another step back and glared at him as if her unplanned confession was all his fault.

"Good luck on your heats," she said, then turned around and strode away.

"Same, Kasey," Peter called after her, wondering how he could've handled that conversation better.

"Don't mind her. She can be a pain in the neck." Peter looked up to see Russell riding up.

"She's moody, anyway," Peter replied. "Where's she from? I mean, before Copperton?" Even as he asked the question, he realized he was breaking his own rule not to get friendly with the two locals that were his biggest rivals on the racecourse. They were locals, after all, and locals and weekenders don't mix. But Russell was talking to him.

"Medicine Hat, Alberta," he replied. "She won lots of races around there but doesn't know anything about the bigger scene. Kids want autographs from her 'cause there are basically no other girls her age who race. Girls have it easy."

Peter forced a half-smile because Russell seemed to expect him to. But he was still registering the fact that both Kasey and Russell had spoken to him. Of course, not while Micah was around.

"Ten minutes to get to the staging area," Russell advised him, slinging a leg over his bike and pedaling away.

Peter figured the top of the podium today should be a toss-up between himself and Micah—Russell being a possible threat, too. Peter really wanted that first place money. He needed it badly for the new rim and forks he needed, not to mention magic trick materials. Second place paid nothing. Micah had no way of knowing how much Peter needed first place, nor would he ever believe a weekender like Peter would need money. In fact, Micah probably needed it more. But that wasn't Peter's problem; it was all a matter of who was the better racer.

Peter shook himself out of his reverie and pointed his bike toward the staging area. He saw his parents waving at him. He waved back and looked around for Jake.

"There you are, and you got the bike," he said. "Good luck, old buddy."

"Same," Jake replied, pulling his demo bike into the staging area.

"Holeshot's all mine," Micah informed Peter from behind.

Peter swung around, not expecting Micah to speak to him, even if he was just trying to mess with Peter's confidence. But competitive racers often did that, and Peter wasn't the kind to be fazed.

"We'll see," Peter tossed back. He snuck a peek at Russell, knowing that Russell was probably just as determined to take the lead early on. Russell's face was tensed up. He remained looking straight ahead.

The stager called out the lane assignments and the

boys slid their bikes onto the gate. While the announcer introduced the moto, the riders clipped their shoes into their pedals and waited for the starter to begin the automated call. Peter rolled his wrists forward in anticipation. He was pleased Kasey had helped him on the best way to handle the triple jump. Might be his only edge against Micah, maybe Russell too.

"Riders ready. Watch the lights." The lights flashed: red, yellow, green. The gate dropped.

Dust rose, people cheered, pedals churned. Peter locked his eyes on the first curve and gunned for the holeshot. As the lineup spread out behind him, he found himself in second place, behind Micah. He set his sights on overtaking Micah within the next thirty seconds—somewhere on the corners, straights, or rhythm section.

Peter aced the step-up, owned the tabletop, and dared to speed up on the corner. He did a low-to-the-ground leap up the next step-up—beautiful, if he could say so himself. His hands vibrated with the bike; his nostrils breathed in dust. The din of the crowd seemed distant. Only the roller-coaster ride of dirt track ahead existed for him. The track, and Micah's bike, which he had to pass.

By the time he was psyching himself up for the triple, he was less than two bike lengths behind Micah's tail. Double manual, he reminded himself. *I can do* that. But as his front tire rose, he noticed that Micah was clearing the entire triple—something way harder to pull off than a double manual, and exactly what Kasey had said Micah had advised Russell not to do. As Peter's front tire dropped at the top of the second dirt hill, exactly according to plan, Micah landed his bike without a waver on the far side of the third, stormed the difficult curve beyond, then rocketed away.

Sneaky, Peter thought, fuming. Did Kasey purposefully give me bad advice, maybe to please Micah so he'd be nicer to her?

Teeth gritted, Peter accelerated down the backside of the triple, finessed the curve, and sped into the rhythm section of bone-jarring, speed-bump-like hillocks. He let his bike hop-touch-hop-touch. Micah might have widened his lead with that maneuver, but Peter was feeling in command and knew anything could happen before the final straight.

Chest heaving, calves burning, the tips of his fingers tingling with excitement, he pumped his legs like his life depended on passing Copperton's ice-cream server. As he came into the straight, he realized with a bolt of panic that Russell was nearly abreast on his left.

"No way, no way," rang in his head as Russell pulled past.

He poured it on like he'd never poured it on. Just feet from the finish line, Russell made the classic mistake of lowering himself to his seat, which allowed Peter to power up to him.

Even as they crossed the finish line, Peter wondered whether he and Russell had tied. He pulled off his helmet and cleared the sweat running down his face.

Kasey's father came on the megaphone. "First place, Micah Rubenson. Second place, Peter Montpetit. Third place, Russell Allen. Wow, what a tight finish. Let's hear it, folks, for these hard-riding boys."

Breathing hard, Peter let the adrenalin ease out of him. Second place, sandwiched between Micah and Russell. Okay, he could live with that for the first go-round. But just wait till the main event.

He hung out near the finish, cheering Jake in like a one-man cheerleading squad, shouting and leaping about. Jake pulled up with sweat streaming down his face and a big smile. "You're pretty loud when you want to be, aren't you?"

"You were awesome the last bit," Peter said.

"Not bad for a newbie on a strange bike, anyway. You got second place," Jake said, looking to see how Peter felt about it.

"But second to none next time," Peter responded, doing a high-five with his friend.

They turned as Russell biked past toward the refreshment stand. "Nice riding," he called out, looking at both of them.

"Thanks," Jake replied. "Same."

Russell nodded as he biked out of earshot.

"You're talking to the other side," Peter half-joked.

"And they're talking to us," Jake said with no smile attached. "What have you got against them, really?"

10   Nailing It

J ake and Peter ate their lunches late in the day on a bench along the track while watching the girls prepare for their main, or final event.

"So, Kasey won two of her three heats," Jake commented.

"Yup, by a big margin," Peter said, having checked the main-event qualifier list.

"By a wide margin on everyone but the girl who beat her the third heat," Jake corrected him.

"Yeah, some girl from Ottawa. Ever heard of her? I don't know the Canadian racers," Peter said.

"Caroline something. She's a name back east, doesn't usually show up at western events. Family must be on vacation around here or something."

"Well, Kasey beat her two out of three rounds," Peter said defensively.

"Who cares?" Jake replied a little too harshly.

Peter ignored that and turned to study the lineup. He felt butterflies in his stomach as he watched Kasey clip in. Her face was so serious, so focused. She took no sideways glances at the other girls in the lineup. When the gates dropped, she tore out at high speed and clinched the holeshot, continuing beyond the bend as a white blur.

"There they go," Jake commented casually, biting into his submarine sandwich. But Peter had set his sandwich down on the bench. He sprang up and elbowed his way through the crowds for a good view of the entire track. He glued his eyes on Kasey. She's not bad, he thought. Not bad at all. He wanted to see what Kasey did on the triple jump. That's where she'd advised him, via Micah, to double manual through the dips and not jump it. Was she good enough to jump it? He'd asked around and learned that neither she nor her main competitor had jumped it during their three qualifying heats. In other words, she'd followed Micah's advice, as had Russell, he'd found out. So she'd probably been truthful about overhearing Micah's chat with Russell.

Coming up to the triple jump, he saw that Caroline whoever from Ottawa was on Kasey's tail. Kasey had to know it. He didn't envy her the pressure. She should take the risk of trying to clear the triple all in one, he thought. Especially if there was a chance her rival would do it.

He found himself tensing up, squeezing his fists like he was on her bike. Jump it, do it, clear it all, he wanted to shout, but she wouldn't have heard him. He saw a quick jerk of her head backwards; she was checking out how close Caroline was. Caroline was barely a spoke behind. He saw Kasey's bike take to the air. She was going for it, going for it! Way up, up and over, like a white stallion with wings. She was aiming for the far side of the last berm. Just a little short, but she might still land it cleanly, he judged. Gutsy girl.

"Go Kasey!" he shouted, jumping up and down, his encouragement drowned out by the crowd's same excitement. Caroline, he noted with a knot in his stomach, was also going for it. She was crouched and ready even before Kasey landed her back tire. Kasey was leaning hard, setting her front tire down, leaning again as her bike jerked her around. She almost got it back under control. She was so very close. But she didn't quite have it; her front tire jack-knifed and folded beneath her.

"No!" Peter cried, placing his hands on either side of his head and willing Caroline to jump short.

The cloud of dirt above Kasey's spill prompted an "oooooohhh" from the crowd, and a corner official scrambled up to warn riders to steer clear. But Caroline was already airborne.

"No!" Peter protested again, taking hold of the chain-link fence in front of him and rattling it wildly.

Caroline landed a touch too long, wobbled nearly as much as Kasey, and came nearly as close to eating dirt. But somehow, she straightened it out and carried on. Meanwhile, the next rider was too late to catch the official's warning, and went down hard. That caused an instant pileup. Bikes, pedals, arms, and legs tangled in a dusty cloud, creating a true spectacle for the audience. As the riders attempted frantically to disentangle themselves and rejoin the race, Kasey managed to make up some of her lost time. She pumped her pedals like a machine. But Caroline had too much on her by then. It wasn't even close, but at least when Kasey crossed the finish line she'd clinched second place.

"Motos ten through twenty report to the staging area," the megaphone voice was urging.

"That's us, Peter! Hurry!" Jake said, coming up behind him. "Forget the girls. Concentrate on your own run!"

Right, his own run. His need to beat Micah for a whole bunch of reasons he didn't have time to think about right now.

Once again, Peter clipped in alongside Russell and Micah. Then he nodded at Jake, who'd made the main, thanks largely to a pileup that had doused the chances of some lead riders. They'd been holding back in their qualifying heats to save their energy for the main, and the plan had backfired. He studiously ignored the Copperton boys.

The sign flashed five, and everyone steadied themselves on their pedals. This time, when the gates dropped, Peter rocketed so fast into the turn he cut off Micah. Coming around the second bend, he was now in the lead. Speed, speed, speed, he told himself. Do everything right, but keep that speed up. Triple jump, triple jump. Can I do it? Yes, no, yes, no. He could feel sweat trickling down his back, but every facet of his existence was locked onto pumping his legs, leaning in the turns, raising his body for the more jarring parts of the route. Triple coming up. Forget who's behind you. Just do what you can do. Do what you can do.

Kasey's failed attempt flashed across his goggles. He decided to play it safe, admitting for once that he simply wasn't skilled enough to risk flying over the entire triple. Instead, just before reaching the crest of the first bump, he double-manualed: pulled back with his arms and kicked his feet forward in the first, then the second dip. It required a fearsome grip on the bars to steady them, and shot adrenalin through his legs as they acted like shock absorbers. But he knew those leg kicks bought him forward momentum. By the far side of the third hump, he was hurling his body forward and using gravity to pick up yet more speed. There he lowered his head and pumped for his life—his life, his prize money, his honor, his whatever.

Behind him, Jake would later tell him, Micah went flying over the entire triple. But Micah cased his tire coming down and only barely recovered before the big curve.

Near the finish, Peter could sense someone behind him, but he was determined that no one would catch him this round. He called on everything he had, lifting his head only after his front tire crossed the finish line. First place! He raised his sweat-soaked, juiced-out arms and tasted victory.

There might have been cheers, but they sounded far away. There might have been congratulatory slaps across the back, but he was too spent to respond. Not till Jake rode in, then circled around to hug him did he regain his breath and his ability to step off the bike with his head held high.

"You did it, man," Jake shouted. "You're No. 1!"

Peter clapped Jake on the back. "And you did way better than you expected."

Jake was nodding with vigor and beaming. "That demo's a nice bike."

Peter looked around and spotted Kasey not many yards away. She was sitting in a folding chair beside her dad's car, her face in her hands. Her dad was towering over her, talking to her. No, scolding her. The jerk. Not far from them, a crowd of little girls was pressed around Caroline.

"Give me a minute to talk to Kasey?" Peter asked Jake. "I'll meet you back at our tent in a minute."

"Sure," Jake said cheerfully and walked away.

Peter edged toward Kasey, wondering what to say. Then he saw her father look up, notice the girls clutched around Caroline, and call out to them.

"Girls," he said, lifting a small brown paper bag over his head. "I've got some free key chains for you."

"Dad," Kasey hissed, raising her head in horror. But her father pretended he hadn't heard her. He took one keychain out and jingled it like he was Santa Claus passing out candy canes. "Free key chains, and they glow in the dark!"

Peter pressed himself into the deep shadow of a building. He watched two of the smallest girls look up and wander over to Kasey. Caroline, busy signing an autograph, had the grace not to raise her head. Was Mr. Lowe for real? Poor Kasey.

"Kasey started training when she was your age," Mr. Lowe was telling the girls, who were accepting the key chains and looking at them dubiously. "You keep it up and you'll be winning as much as her. Did you see her almost take first?"

Peter shrank even further into the shadows as Kasey raised her head. Her face was lined in misery. Without looking at Caroline or the girls in front of her, she stood up and started answering the girls' questions mechanically, like a programmed robot. Short, vague smiles gave Peter the impression she was weary—or embarrassed—enough to collapse. It would be easy, Peter thought, for someone to think that her lack of enthusiasm, or the cool distance she put between herself and her fans, meant she was stuck-up, a poor loser, or both. But as Peter looked from Kasey to Mr. Lowe, he saw a princess with frizzy red hair, locked in a tower, a princess desperate to live up to her father's dreams for her.

"You just wait till she makes national champ," Mr. Lowe was telling the girls. "Those autographs you got from her will be valuable."

Kasey lowered her head at that. Her blue eyes were hidden by her thick eyelashes. Peter could sense the anger and rebellion she was struggling, and succeeding for now, to keep down.

She'd won second place and given one of Canada's best a true run for her money. So she was skilled, she had potential, but was her heart in it? She needed to love the sport to get to the next level. Her father couldn't make her love it. No coach could make her love it. Did her dad know that?

"Get out of here before Kasey sees you," Peter told himself. Reluctantly, he turned and ran.

As he searched for Jake, he spotted his parents showing a young couple the family's BMW. Had his parents asked him before they'd decided to sell the car? No! Those people had better not be thinking about buying it.

"Want a hot dog?" Jake asked as he came around the corner of the refreshment stand with two sports drinks in his hand.

"Nah, that's okay," Peter said, accepting the drink, unscrewing its cap, and tipping the bottle to his lips.

"I still can't believe you got first prize!" Jake enthused. "So, what're you going to do with the money? Buy me a bike, maybe?" He laughed and punched Peter lightly on the shoulder.

"Taking you and my folks out for ice cream, of course," Peter replied as he watched Micah standing near the triple jump, staring at it with hunched shoulders. "And I'll give the server a really big tip."

"I don't think that will go over well at all," Jake said cautiously. "You know Micah would be insulted. He's an okay guy. There's nothing wrong with him not liking outsiders. Don't make him into an enemy, Peter." Jake paused when Peter didn't respond, but Peter had shifted his gaze to his parents and the couple looking over his car. "You're joking about the big tip, right?" Jake pressed.

Peter hadn't been joking, and he knew Jake was right. But he didn't care. Nope, he didn't care one bit. Anyway, Micah probably needed the money. Micah was lucky Peter was a generous guy. Peter didn't like Micah and he wasn't going to pretend otherwise. The guy was a local, Peter was not, and that was that.

Want to live in a small town again. Get back to my roots, you know?

"No!" Peter responded so forcefully that Jake flinched, but Peter had already forgotten Jake's question.

11   Hardware Store

J ake grabbed the knot at the end of the rope and swung out over the lake.

"Cowabunga!" he shouted as he let go and dropped into the clear blue water. He relished the cool wetness against his sweaty body. He pointed his toes, letting his body slice down, down, down. As it slowed to a stop, he hung there in the deep coolness, relaxed, happy. But the bevy of bubbles around him was already lifting him gently upward. His compressed lungs told him to raise his arms and kick his legs—kick back up to the sunshine, back to the view of the stony hills around him, back to where he could breathe.

He burst to the surface and did a relaxed backstroke as he watched Peter on the low cliff above fold his hands around the rope's knot and grin down. The sun glinted off something on Peter's wrists, but by the time Jake shaded his eyes and realized Peter was wearing handcuffs, Peter was already in midair.

Jake's mouth fell open as he treaded water faster, wondering what he should do. Peter plunged in. Jake began to count. One, two … By the time he got to forty-five, he was plunging his head underwater, surfacing, diving again. There was no sign of Peter in the deep lake. With his heart pounding in his chest, Jake sucked in the deepest breath he could and dove deep. Frantically, his hands worked the water to take him down to where it was dark and cold. Down, down he went until his ears ached and his lungs screamed. This time, he barely made it back to the surface in time to breathe. And there was Peter, grinning like a madman, suspended in the water with the opened handcuffs lifted above his wet curly blond hair.

"You're going to kill yourself, Peter," Jake gasped. "And me. This is going too far. I'm going to burn every last one of your Houdini and Blaine books."

Peter's smile faded slowly. He looked hurt. He lowered the handcuffs. "Jake, stop being a worrywart. I know what I'm doing. You know how long I can hold my breath. You know I've been training my lungs in the bathtub at the cabin. And you know how fast I can pick locks; you've been timing me. So what's to worry about? I had the handcuffs open right away. From two little pieces of wire I hid in my swim trunks."

"You're not supposed to tell how you do magic tricks."

"Who cares? Anyway, I had to stay down as long as I could for the audience effect, and as part of my lung capacity training. So relax, okay? Want to time me while I do it again?"

"No!" Jake said forcefully. Suddenly, he didn't feel like swimming at all.

"Once Houdini was dumped into water while handcuffed and squeezed into a wooden crate. The crate was held shut with nails, heavy rope, and metal bands. And he escaped, no problem. And Blaine survived being buried for a week—"

"I don't want to know," Jake said, picturing Peter burying himself and staying hidden there until his parents got jobs again and everything seemed normal to his stubborn mind. "Let's go to the hardware store. I need some chain lube."

Peter looked disappointed but didn't argue. "Okay, and I'm going to stop at the library on the way."

They found Kasey minding the store for her dad. Jake couldn't help but notice her downcast eyes and flat greeting. She looked bummed out. After she'd pointed him to the bike parts section, Jake overheard Peter try to chat with her. Jake couldn't help listening in.

"So, congrats on placing second at the race. Haven't seen you since then."

"Thanks."

"Haven't seen you on the course at all. Can't coach you if you're not there. What's up?"

"I'm not going to race anymore," the answer came in a distracted tone.

"What? But you took second, nearly got first. You were awesome. And all the girls around here look up to you."

"Kids only want my autograph because there's no other girls around, hardly. I'm not all that interested in racing anymore."

"What, are you kidding, Kasey? But you're good."

"I'm not that good. Dad just thinks I am. Besides, try being stuck in this town with only Micah and Russell to bike with. They're so bossy, and they only pretend to be my friends."

Peter was quiet for a moment. Jake reached for the chain lube squeeze bottle. So, he thought, she is capable of being humble sometimes.

"You can bike with us anytime you want, Kasey," Peter said. "You don't have to bike with those losers—or do everything they say."

Kasey tossed her head. "Oh yeah? That's what you think. You're weekenders. You'll be gone again in a few weeks. Anyway, what do you want out of pretending you'd like to bike with me?"

"What do I want? Nothing, Kasey."

Yeah right, Jake thought to himself at the same time as Kasey said it aloud.

"Okay, maybe there is something I'd like. Something I'd appreciate, if you're willing," Peter corrected himself.

"Permission to bike at the racetrack," Kasey guessed.

"Well, that too maybe, but that's not the main thing."

"I'm listening," Kasey responded. Jake peeked through the shelves and saw her crossing her arms. If she didn't want to race anymore, that made her a bad loser, didn't it? And she'd only been using Peter to get coaching while she was interested in racing, just like Peter had agreed just for access to the course. Or was something else going on here?

"Will you let us bike in the tunnels with you?" Peter asked uncertainly.

Kasey burst out laughing. "What, you've got night-vision goggles and an oxygen meter now? And you think I know all the routes? I only know one. On the rest, I just follow Micah. And there's no way he'll ever take you into the tunnels."

A bell rang as a customer entered the store, and Peter roamed the aisles until he found Jake.

"Who wants to bike in the tunnels?" Jake demanded in a raspy whisper. "Not me, and not you if you have any sense. Or have you already forgotten what happened last week?"

"Shhh. I have a plan. Want to see what I got at the library?"

Jake sighed. "Dunno. Do I?"

Peter tugged a folded piece of paper out of his shorts pocket as the customer exited the store and Kasey joined them.

"Hey," she said. "That's a map of the tunnels, just like Micah's. Where'd you get that?"

"Library. History section. It's from when the mine was operating. And look at this," Peter said, pulling a calculator out of his other pocket.

Wait, Jake thought. That's not a calculator. It's …

"An oxygen meter!" Kasey exclaimed, then glanced about to make sure her customer had left and no one else was in the store. "Micah give you that?" Then she made a face. "Like that's even a possibility."

"No, I bought it off eBay. There it was, like it was waiting for me. Waiting for us. And here it is!" Peter said proudly. "Put a dent in my savings, even at half-price, but we'll be working soon, Jake. I want to bike in the tunnels. Come on, admit it. You'd like to, too. It'd be the ultimate in cool and scary. You thought Copperton was boring. But now we've found something exciting. You've always liked doing risky, adventurous stuff."

It was true. Jake could be talked into doing the tunnels if they had the safety equipment. Biking in the tunnels with night-vision goggles and an oxygen meter would be just too cool to imagine, even if it was still a bit risky. But he wouldn't do it without all the right gear and someone to show them the ropes.

"Me too," Kasey spoke up unexpectedly, her eyes dancing. "Biking in the tunnels is the most exciting thing I've ever done. There's like hundreds of tunnels under that hill. It's way better than racing, and my dad has no idea I'm doing it." Her gleeful tone was in stark contrast to what they'd heard when they'd entered the store. Was it riding in the tunnels she liked, or defying her overbearing father?

"Exactly!" Peter enthused, looking at Kasey approvingly. "So, all we need now are some night-vision goggles. Kasey, do you know where we can get some?" Peter asked. "They sell 'em on the Net, but they're way too expensive."

Kasey's good mood melted into sudden suspicion. She placed her hands on her hips and squinted her clear blue eyes.

"Whoa, what was I thinking? So, you expect me to just walk up to Micah and Russell and say, hey, my new friends want to go riding in the tunnels, can I borrow your night-vision goggles? For a minute there I'd convinced myself you were different but you're just a typical weekender, out for what you can get. You blow into town for one or two weeks a year, ignore the locals unless there's something you need, ride around in your silver BMW and on your fancy racing bike. Swim in our lake—the one no one around here can afford to live on because of what you've done to land prices. Drop into our BMX race, grab all the awards 'cause you have better bikes, better training, more time and money to run around the race circuit. And now you think I'm just going to hand you night-vision goggles so you can bike in our secret places. All because you think Kasey Lowe is a loser in need of someone to ride with!"

She turned on her heel and stomped off to a back-room, her red frizz vibrating with anger.

Peter looked at Jake. Jake looked at Peter. Jake dared not say anything. Lots of what Kasey said was true—true about Peter and the weekenders. Peter needed to hear it, needed to realize what image he projected with the fancy racing bike, the BMW, the cabin, and the way he talked to and about locals. And he needed to see he was clinging to the belief he had money to throw around and the locals didn't, even though it wasn't true anymore.

And Peter didn't appreciate the dilemma this would create for Kasey. They would be gone in a couple of weeks and then she'd be here alone. Micah and Russell may not be ideal friends for Kasey, but they were her age and they shared an interest in BMXing. Peter needed to put his dislike of Micah aside and not use Kasey in his war against the guy. So what if Peter and Micah were rivals on the race scene? Sure Micah was bossy. All groups had a natural leader, and that's what Micah was for the local bikers. Lately, Jake had found himself warming up to the muscular biker a little. He was smart and confident, qualities Jake admired.

And Jake, knowing what it was like not to have tons of money, could sympathize with the grudge Micah had against weekenders. They had easier access to jobs, nice cars, lots around the lake, whatever. He wondered why Peter couldn't understand that his superior attitude just gave Micah more reason to dislike weekenders. There must be something else about the mine manager's son that was setting Peter off and Jake hadn't figured it out.

Jake watched Peter sigh and walk over to where the chains were sold. He fingered several sizes before selecting one and drawing a length slowly off its spool. The squeak of the turning spool brought Kasey out again, checking to see if a new customer was in the store. Her eyes were slightly puffy; her eyelashes were wet. She looked surprised to see Jake and Peter still there.

"I need to pay for this chain lube," Jake said hesitantly, laying it down gently on the counter. "And I'm really sorry you feel that way about weekenders, though I can't say I blame you."

She sniffed and rang in the chain lube without looking at him, but her face seemed to be mellowing. By the time she'd handed him his change, she looked at him with no anger in her features.

"Stupid, isn't it? I thought it was stupid when we first moved here, and here I am sounding like Micah, who grew up here. He blames weekenders for the mine shutting down."

"Huh? What do weekenders have to do with that?" Jake asked.

"Nothing. Dad said it was to do with the copper market taking a dive. But Micah thinks it's to do with weekenders driving up real estate prices. He blames them for his dad not having a job, for him having to help support his dad, for his dad drinking in the bar all day. And Russell's got the same chip on his shoulder about the army base shutting down."

She looked up as Peter approached the counter with his chain.

"I'm sorry, Kasey," Peter said with his head lowered. "I've never understood the locals-versus-weekenders thing."

Ha! As if, Jake thought. He totally understands it. He's been coming to his cabin for years and was perfectly happy not to mix with locals till he wanted on that racetrack and knew Kasey was his ticket there. Now he's trying to smooth talk her by pretending he's never known about the issue. Peter sure was a cool customer, but what was it all for?

"Look, I don't want to put you in a gnarly spot with Micah and Russell, and I'm sorry. But they don't need to know, just like your dad doesn't need to know. Micah and Russell may be right about us weekenders, but that doesn't mean this should stop us being friends." He gestured to the three of them. "I still want to bike with you. On the course, or on our dirt jumps, around town, wherever. Just forget what I said about the tunnels and night-vision goggles."

Jake was surprised to feel a stab of disappointment about the tunnel riding but impressed that Peter had apologized. What surprised him most, however, was Kasey's smile.

"Know what?" she asked.

"What?" Jake and Peter asked together.

"I'm tired of doing everything Micah says just so he'll start being nicer to me. You know, he only ever coaches Russell because Russell thinks Micah's some kind of hero."

"Russell's a really good rider. He doesn't need Micah's help," Jake declared. "He should learn to stand up to Micah."

Kasey nodded. "We all should. You know what else?"

"What?"

"I know where Russell has hidden that box of old night-vision goggles he found in the dump." Her freckled face took on a sly look and she chuckled. "We'll have to make sure we return them to the hiding place when we're not using them and hope he doesn't notice. But what the heck, it's worth the risk. I'll come tunnel-biking with you sometime. Wow, if they knew ..." Her lips curled into a menacing grin, her hands returned to her hips, and she tossed her head. "That will be $19.39 for the chain, Mr. Montpetit. Paper or plastic?"

12   Night Vision

J ake pulled the goggles on and whistled a low whistle. "Is this cool or what? Like a video game but real. Everything's green-like."

"I was afraid you weren't going to join us," Peter said as he and Kasey mounted their bikes just ahead of him inside the tunnel entrance.

"Are you kidding?" Jake exclaimed. "I wouldn't miss this. If we've got a map, an oxygen meter, night-vision goggles, and an experienced guide, how could there be a problem?"

"Hey, I should charge you for my experienced guiding," Kasey joked as she tightened the chinstrap on her helmet.

"How do these things work, anyway?" Peter asked her as they adjusted the eyepieces on their goggles.

"They wouldn't work if we didn't have lights on our bikes," Kasey informed them. "The goggles take that light and make it more intense, including light wavelengths we can't see with our eyes."

"Cool. Can't believe the army dumped these," Jake said as the three began riding.

"Guess the new ones are more technologically advanced," said Kasey, her voice echoing a little. "Russell's always combing the dump and the old army base for stuff. But this was quite the find."

Widening her lead on the boys, Kasey unexpectedly burst into song ahead of them.

> *Where day is dark, and midnight hours are bright*
> *With strange unearthly gleams of lurid light*
> *Then a sweet voice shall fill this enchanted maze,*
> *Unveil mysteries of ancient days.*

Her perfect pitch and impressive voice range pierced the darkness of the tunnel. She's good, Jake thought. Very good. He let the music mesmerize him for a few moments. Despite the lyrics, his apprehension about the place melted away.

> *With trembling hearts we leave the upper light,*
> *And travel downwards to the realms of night,*
> *With wondering eyes we watch the sunlight die,*
> *And stars beam mildly in a noontide sky.*

"Where's that song from?" Jake asked.

"Found it in a book called *Caverns of Night*. Epic name, eh? It's about coal mining."

Her voice trailed off when she glanced back to see that Peter had paused at the fork where things had gone wrong last time. Peter peered up the steep ramp with his goggle eyes. "I don't see any tunnel goblins waiting to thunk me on the head," he said.

"Come on. We know not to go up there," Jake said quickly.

"Wrong. I have to go up there," Peter responded, hopping off his bike and taking a few steps up the ramp.

"Peter! That's the wrong way. I'm guiding here!" Kasey objected as Jake prepared to leap off his bike and grab Peter.

Peeeep. A high-pitched chirping echoed off the walls.

"Good stuff. It works." Peter stopped in his tracks and pushed a button on the oxygen meter in his hand to reset it. "Important to test these things. Remember how twelve miners died in Sago, West Virginia, because they hadn't tested their emergency oxygen packs first? Only one guy survived."

"I know one way worse than that," Kasey piped up as Peter walked back to his bike. "1862. Northumberland in northern England: 204 miners buried alive. They were trying to dig themselves out same time as the rescuers were digging like crazy, trying to reach them. The rescuers could hear the men for the longest time. Then it got quieter and quieter, until they heard nothing. When they finally broke through to where the miners were, all 204 were dead."

"That's horrible!" Peter said as he and Kasey started moving forward again.

Jake just shivered as he pedaled behind them in the shadowy passageway. He preferred Kasey's singing. And he had decided she was okay, really.

"A bunch of them had written notes to their families," she continued. "One carved a message on his tin flask: 'My dear Sara—I leave you.'"

She burst into another verse of her song:

Then first is heard the moaning of despair,
And then the sad farewell and muttered prayer,
And many a spirit from this gloomy night
Is borne aloft to realms of purest light.

"Okay," Jake interjected. "Enough of that. Bad luck to tell stories or sing songs like that in here."

"Jake's a worrywart," Peter informed Kasey.

"A worrywart who's saved your butt a couple of times," Jake reminded Peter, flashing back to the way he'd had to drag Peter down the ramp.

"True enough. My turn to be a hero next," Peter teased.

They came to another fork, where Kasey kept left. The smooth, damp walls glistened an eerie, phosphorescent green through Jake's funny eyepieces. He suddenly realized why Russell liked the tunnels. One could imagine being on a special army mission in hostile territory at night. Moving stealthily with his M16 cocked and ready, he watched for telltale movement or that weird neon-green identifying a warm body lying in wait for him.

Jake began to relax and have fun, like Peter and Kasey. The three would take turns doing flatlander tricks: "hitchhikers" and "decades" and "bus drivers." They even did grinds on the occasional left-behind segment of steel rail. Occasionally, there would be an accumulation of dirt against a wall. Just enough to let Jake run up it like it was a ramp, catch a little air, test some new tricks he was trying out.

Three times, Kasey slowed down and raised her hand to indicate they needed to stop.

"Mine shaft coming up," she would say. "We have to get off our bikes and walk along the side rim—I mean that wood frame around it—while holding our bikes. Grip those iron bars on the wall with one hand so you don't fall in."

Jake and Peter would peer down these square black

holes with interest. They were like giant manholes—the size of a large service elevator, maybe eight by eight feet square—with iron ladders bolted along one side, disappearing into the darkness. The wood frame around the shafts was about the width of Jake's shoe. Which means it was like walking along a wooden tightrope with a twenty-pound bike in one hand, the other trying to feel for an iron handhold sunk into a dark, clammy rock wall. Cool.

One shaft provided more than just a frame around it. Workers hadn't gotten around to pulling out two bars of steel across it: rail spans. But since there were no cross-ties between the thin, slippery metal rails, they couldn't use them as a bridge. They ended up edging around the side rims just like the others. But Jake paused to stare at the steel rails for a moment. They looked lonely, even ghostly, suspended in time.

"Did miners have to climb up and down the shafts to get from one tunnel to another?" Peter asked Kasey.

"Only in an emergency," Kasey replied. "Back when this place was running, there'd be cables for a hoist and cage—that's miner talk for an elevator—running up and down some of the shafts. Russell just found a big metal grill at the dump that we're going to haul in here. Then we can bike across at least one shaft easier."

"How many tunnels are there?" Jake asked as

they continued to stare down the shaft as if gathered around a deep well.

"No idea, but I know that lots of them are like five miles long. The deepest tunnels are almost a mile underground. There'd be air pumped down there."

Jake tried to imagine climbing one mile of ladders in a mining emergency.

"The newest tunnels are at the bottom. The oldest ones are up top," Kasey continued in her tour-guide voice. "In the early days they started 'em near the surface—and just kept going down farther each year. At least, that's what Micah says."

Jake watched Kasey skirt around the hole while carrying her bike. She waited for the boys to do the same. A metal grill hauled in here from the dump and placed underfoot would be way safer and easier, he thought.

"Why is Micah so into this place?" Jake asked once he and Peter had climbed back on their bikes.

Kasey looked thoughtful for a moment. "You mean besides the fact that it's fun and secret and a little bit dangerous? He wanted to work here," Kasey said. "All his relatives worked the mines. They're always telling him stories about the place and he likes to go to the library and read about it. He keeps saying his dad was happy here. Maybe that's why Micah likes this place. 'Cause his dad sure isn't happy these days."

"I thought mining was supposed to be a horrible job," Jake objected. "Hard work, filthy, dangerous, unhealthy." He blinked and sniffed the air. Biking down here for fun was one thing. But working here every day of your life?

Kasey shrugged. "Yeah, but it's a job. And if it's how everyone in your family earned a living, and then suddenly it's gone and your dad doesn't have a job, you'd probably think differently. He's always talking about how it's going to be opened up again one day."

She slung her leg over her bike with a look that implied she was afraid she'd said too much. Jake thought about Peter's dad, wondered what was going through Peter's mind right now. Richard Montpetit had probably always been happy at their Copperton cabin before now. But what had seemed like a rock-solid lifestyle was falling apart for the family these days.

Peter raised his feet to his pedals. "We've been in here a long time. And I sure don't want my parents sending out a search party. Can you lead us out now, Kasey?"

"Sure. We don't need to backtrack. I know a route out from here."

They stood in silence and Jake realized he was thinking about doors and openings and fresh air. "So you guys broke through plugs blocking the tunnel entrances?" he asked.

"Yup," Kasey replied in a low voice, hanging her

head for a second. "It took awhile chipping through the concrete blocks, even if they're hollow and we only went for old, crumbling ones."

"Russell said there were some with timber plugs. Wouldn't those have been easier to break through?" Jake asked.

"I guess," Kasey said, shrugging. "We just do what Micah says."

Jake adjusted his goggles and followed Kasey and Peter around a few more twists, ups, and downs. Suddenly, the greenish walls exploded into blinding white. Jake tore his goggles off, squeezed his eyes shut, then opened them. Relief flooded through his body. Kasey had found an exit.

13　Chains

P eter couldn't believe how quickly the blood rushed to his head, how crushed his chest felt, how his legs threatened to all but separate from his body at the hips. He was hanging by his feet from a giant hook in the garage ceiling, wrapped in two sets of chains secured with three different kinds of locks.

"Stopwatch ready?" he asked Jake, who was lounging in a lawn chair, paging through BMX magazines.

"Sure," Jake replied, reluctantly lifting his eyes from the article he was reading.

"You can't watch me, you know. You have to look the other way."

"Why? You're going to tell me how you did it afterwards anyway. You always do."

"Doesn't matter. Houdini never let anyone watch him close up. He usually did this trick while hanging from the top of a tall building. Made it more exciting for the spectators on the ground, but also kept them from seeing exactly how he escaped."

"Well, I'm glad there are no tall buildings around here," Jake replied, giving the stopwatch a quick test. "But other than that, you're doing it the same way as Houdini?"

"No way. I can't. Know how Houdini used to escape from chains and straitjackets?"

"Hid a pair of scissors and bolt cutters up his nose?" Jake joked.

"Nope. He dislocated both shoulders and put them back in again so fast, no one knew. Not too many people can do that."

Jake shook his head. "Uh, no, I'll bet not too many can. Peter, you are seriously whacked. We're meeting Kasey at the track after this, right? Can't believe you actually talked her into a practice when she doesn't want to race anymore."

"Wasn't that hard to talk her into it. It's not like there's a lot else to do in Copperton. Anyway, let's get this show on the road. I'm hungry. I need to get out of these chains and eat lunch!"

Jake nodded and raised the stopwatch. "Ready, set …"

The phone startled both boys out of their anticipation and Peter groaned. His chains rattled as he shifted in his heavy cocoon. "Not now!" But they'd had to bring the phone into the garage with them while his mom ran an errand—his mom's orders. She was expecting a call from Peter's dad, who'd driven down to Seattle for a job interview. He'd looked really good all dressed up in a suit that morning. Really good, and he'd been smiling. Peter's mom had even gone all out to make them a big, fancy breakfast as a send-off.

"It's probably Dad telling us he got the job," Peter said confidently. Everything would be okay now. It was about time. "How about you turn the phone upside down and press it against my ear?"

Jake grinned and did just that.

"Hello. Montpetit residence," Peter spoke into the phone, hoping he didn't sound upside down.

"Who? Oh. Uh-huh." He gritted his teeth and felt more blood drain into his head. "Well, I'm very sorry, but it's not for sale anymore." Jake was looking at him, eyes suddenly narrowed. "Uh-huh. Well, sorry. Good luck. Yup. Bye."

"The cabin?" Jake asked him accusingly.

"Yup," Peter replied. "Dad's probably going to get that job today, and then they'll take it off the market."

He watched Jake fiddle with the stopwatch and struggle to say nothing. It wasn't his business, anyway. No way was Peter going to help his parents sell this cabin when they didn't really need to sell it. It wasn't fair. Nobody had asked him.

"So, I'm ready," he informed Jake.

"Okay. Three, two, one, go!"

Glancing over to make sure that Jake had turned his head away, Peter went into action. Voila, one lock free. Rattle, rattle, grunt. Yes! Second one open. Peter used all his strength to lift his head to the third and highest one.

"No!" Peter shouted as the phone trilled to life again, breaking his concentration. He was always super tense when interrupted in the middle of a really hard trick, especially when it was being timed.

"Hello? Hi, Mr. Montpetit!" Jake was saying. "How'd it go? Sorry, Mrs. Montpetit is out for half an hour, and Peter's tied up at the moment. Can I give them a message?"

Peter was having trouble with the third lock. The blasted thing just wouldn't give, even though he knew he was doing the combination correctly—with his mouth, no less. He couldn't stay in this position much longer, even with all the physical training he'd been doing to make this trick work.

"Oh." Peter couldn't see Jake's face, but he could hear the change of tone. The chains were now feeling intolerably tight. Maybe he hadn't puffed his chest out enough when Jake was wrapping him up. His neck was feeling the strain of trying to hold his upper body in a position where he could get at the last lock.

"Well, I'm real sorry to hear that, Mr. Montpetit. But 200 applicants for one position, that's pretty tough. Never mind. At least you're getting interviews. Next time, for sure. Uh-huh. Okay. Sure, I'll tell him. See you tomorrow. Bye."

Jake set the phone down. He seemed to be having a hard time meeting Peter's eyes. "He didn't get the job. Sorry, Peter. And he said to tell you he's registered you at the public school and—and we're to help your mom clean the cabin tomorrow because there's a showing. Someone interested in buying."

Peter's neck felt like it was going to snap. "I … can't … take … it … any … more!" he shouted, wanting to rip the lock apart with his teeth. He dropped his head all the way, dangling to where his hair was a mere foot above the garage floor. He felt the chains tighten around his body, fought a sense of despair. He'd made his own straitjacket, sewing up the sleeves of a long-sleeved shirt and when his arms were in them, Jake had tied the sleeves behind his back. Maybe that hadn't been a good idea. Maybe he'd gotten himself too trapped. He groaned.

"I give up, Jake. Can't do it." An unreasonable anger was taking over his body. Maybe it was from hanging upside down too long, maybe because he couldn't do magic, maybe because he didn't like being trapped. But his eyes locked on a crowbar lying on the garage floor, and he knew that the minute Jake let him down, he was going to take it in his hands and beat something to a pulp.

14   Crowbars and Tanks

The minute Jake freed Peter, Peter stormed out of the garage, stooping to pick up a crowbar on the way. He grabbed his bike roughly by the handlebars, slung a leg over without looking back, and headed for the hills. "Don't follow me," was all he said, in a husky, half-choked voice.

Did he really expect Jake to stay put? No way was Jake going to let him do something stupid in that dark mood of his. So Jake grabbed his bike and followed close behind, not caring if Peter noticed. He followed Peter up and down faint dirt trails, wondering how long it would take his buddy to calm down, when he'd turn around and talk, and whether he knew where he was going.

"Just what we needed," he called to Peter, "a bike ride. It'll make you feel better."

The hills smelled fresh after a recent rain. Green

saplings washed of dirt reached for the sun. It wouldn't be long before they'd be trees, Jake thought. Trees that might be stunted from growing among the mine tailings, but trees proud to be trees nonetheless.

How long before Peter slowed down and cheered up? Jake wondered. Obviously the news about his dad not getting the job and being taken out of school was a one-two punch he couldn't handle.

After twenty minutes of not once looking behind, Peter slowed, dropped his bike, and headed toward a bush against a nearby rock face.

Birds twittered and a gentle breeze brought the sweet smell of cedar trees to Jake's nose.

Finally, thought Jake. We can sit here and enjoy the view until he's pulled himself together. But to Jake's surprise, Peter lifted the crowbar and struck it violently against something behind the bush. Birds rose and cried in protest. Jake cocked his head and spotted what looked like the remains of a half-rotted gray barn door—a door set into the rock wall.

Peter whacked four times, putting his entire upper body into it. Jake blinked. It was like a scene from a reality cop show where someone has been ordered to knock down the apartment door of a violent criminal gang member. Jake recoiled from the sound of wood splintering and breaking. He moved closer, mouth hanging open, to see that his high-strung friend was breaking through what was left of the wooden plug of a mine-tunnel entrance.

"Peter!" Jake called out. "What are you doing? That's destruction of private property."

The tool froze in mid-air, then dropped. Peter sank to the ground, hands over his head. "Leave … me … alone," he pleaded in a hollow tone.

Jake hesitated. He'd come this far, and he had reason to be shocked at the way Peter had spent his anger. But who was he to criticize Peter for widening a hole in an already-rotted door, especially when they were both guilty of trespassing in the tunnels now?

"Can't," Jake said gently. "I'm worried about you." Seemed about time he did what was right, not what Peter asked him to do.

Neither said anything for a few minutes. Finally, Peter raised his head. "I feel better now."

Jake relaxed a little. "Thought you might."

Another minute of silence was marked by the boys watching a squirrel scamper from one tree to another. Trees that had decided to grow atop a former mine, a squirrel that had decided to live a hardscrabble life up here. Peter pushed the crowbar away from him like he was ashamed of having used it.

"He's not going to get a job right away, is he?" Peter asked without looking up. "Or Mom."

"It's possible," Jake said softly. "When my dad left,

I thought it was the end of the world. But we ended up being okay. You're a racer, Peter. You know how to suck it up after losing, and you know how to change your training to suit different racecourses."

Peter stared at the crowbar, half nodding. Then he smiled and looked up at the sun.

"I saw a wooden door the other side of that hill that had fallen off its hinges," he said in a voice that sounded like a confession. He wasn't looking at Jake. "I looked on the map to find it, then found the tunnel's other side. Here. But the door here was still holding, even if it was rotted, too."

"So you came here and battered it down so you could explore a new tunnel?" Jake asked with mild alarm, but not surprise.

"Uh-huh," Peter said, burying his face in his hands again. "I'd told myself I wouldn't, 'cause it's not right." He hesitated. "But then I got mad and did."

Jake took a deep breath. "I understand," he said. "But you're not going in there now, right? Just 'cause it's open both ends doesn't mean you have to go in there. Especially alone when you're in this mood."

Peter raised his head and nodded in agreement. "Yeah, I promise."

The two just looked at each other for a few seconds.

"Jake, mind if I go for a long bike ride by myself up here?" Peter asked, his face looking relaxed now.

"No offense, but I kind of need some time on my own right now."

"No problem," Jake said, returning the smile. "Now that you've promised you won't go in there." He pointed at the tunnel entrance.

Peter shook his head. "No, I'm going riding in the sunshine. I need to work on my tan." He smiled weakly.

"Okay." Jake rose, picked up his bike, and jumped on its pedals. "Have a good ride, Peter." And he took off. His light heart, it seemed, made the ride down the steep terrain even faster.

He meant to return to the cabin, but when he saw the silver BMW in the driveway, with its doors wide open to reveal sacks of groceries, he turned impulsively toward town instead. He didn't want to give Laura her husband's phone message yet. Peter would be home soon, and he was the better person to tell her.

Jake rode toward town past the closed-down army base. He peered through the tall rusted fence and saw drab, concrete buildings. He paused to take in their padlocked doors, dark and curtainless windows, and the rolls of barbed wire outlining their flat roofs. Weeds poked up through cracks in the sidewalks of the complex.

He felt sad for Copperton's residents. It had to be lousy living in a dying town. First the mine, now this. His eyes shifted to the Second World War tank that sat just inside the fence at the base's entrance—a monument to wars past, present, and future, and to soldiers proud to serve their country. Soldiers like Russell's dad, who'd probably passed that tank every day on his way to work when he was stationed here. Jake was about to move on when he saw a soldier in green-and-brown fatigues and beret rise from the tank's open hatch. Huh? Thought the place was closed. Jake cycled closer and decided the figure was too small to be a soldier. Somehow, he wasn't surprised when Russell's eyes met his.

"How'd you get in there?" Jake asked Russell, spotting Russell's bike leaning against the side of the tank.

Russell flashed a smile. "Want to sit in the tank?" he asked, eyes sweeping left and right to make sure no one else was around.

"Sure," Jake said.

Russell pointed him to a gap in the fence and helped him pull his bike through it. He gestured for Jake to step on his bike seat to get a handhold that would let him hoist himself to the top of the tank. The minute Jake had dropped through the hatch into the driver's seat, Russell scrambled up onto the tank and landed lightly beside him inside.

Jake couldn't resist touching all the controls even if, like the hatch door above them, they'd long since been decommissioned and frozen in place. He was also keenly aware of the unusually animated figure beside him.

"So, been biking much lately? Tried out the dirt jumps yet?" Jake asked Russell casually, hoping the boy might be conversational without Micah around.

"You bet," Russell replied, and launched into an unexpectedly long-winded description of this week's tunnel, dirt, jump, and racecourse exploits. "Almost beat Micah on a timed practice run," he finished with a sideways grin as he removed his beret and smoothed it between his hands.

"What would've happened if you'd beaten him?" Jake asked.

Russell chuckled and rested his cap back on his shaved head. "It'll never happen," he confided.

"'Cause Micah couldn't live with that?" Jake suggested boldly.

Russell didn't lose his smile, as Jake had expected. He just rested a practiced hand on the controls, grinned, and repeated, "It'll never happen."

"So you're holding yourself back to stay friends with him," Jake said, shaking his head. "I could've sworn at the race practices that he was giving you tips on stuff you could already do as well as him."

Russell shrugged and wriggled into a tiny compartment in the inside rear of the tank.

"Want some gum?" he asked Jake.

"Sure," Jake replied, accepting a stick and curling it into his mouth. "Hey, how'd you get in there?" Jake could hardly imagine getting his head in, let alone squeezing his broad shoulders in.

"I'm little," Russell replied as if it was a point of pride.

Little and agile as a monkey, Jake thought. And okay with taking orders from Micah.

"So how come you and Kasey let Micah boss you around?" Jake heard himself asking, surprised the words had slipped out of his mouth.

Russell scratched his head and ran a finger along the smooth steel plating of the tank's insides. He snapped his gum. Then he looked at Jake with an unflinching, army-style stare. "You mean like you let Peter boss you around?"

Jake felt his face flush hot and red. He hoped the shadows in the tank's belly hid it. Russell was quick and perceptive, Jake realized with growing respect. "Yeah, I have been. He's been going through a tough time. But maybe I'm not doing him any favors being like that."

Russell snapped his gum again. "Micah and I grew up here. We understand what's going down with Copperton. But Micah's got it worse."

"You mean, 'cause his dad doesn't have a job."

Russell nodded. "But maybe I'm not doing him any favors either." He echoed Jake's words, peering at him conspiratorially. Then he looked more serious. "Don't mind Micah and his temper. He gets his nose out of joint easily. But it mends quick—like yours has."

Jake felt his broken nose as Russell's sardonic grin reappeared.

"And don't mind Peter," Jake replied evenly. "He blows hard sometimes, puts his foot in his mouth a lot. But he's okay. Just having a tough summer."

Russell nodded like he understood. "Heard about his dad," he said. "But at least his dad's in town, not getting shot at in the Middle East."

It was Jake's turn to nod. He'd had way too much experience with absent dads himself. "He may even be mellowing," he added, thinking about Peter after the crowbar incident.

"Yeah?" Russell rolled over and slithered out of the compartment with the same mind-boggling limbo moves that got him in there in the first place.

"Want a tour of the base?" he asked, squeezing past Jake to pop his head up out of the hatch and scout the terrain for potential enemies. "There's an empty building where I'm building a sweet half-pipe."

Jake poked his head up out of the hatch, too, and grinned. "Why am I not surprised?"

15　Blazing New Trails

Peter had his feet planted at the tunnel's entrance and was clutching the oxygen meter in his hand, extending it as far in front of him as he could.

"Told you," he said, turning around and holding it toward Jake and Kasey so they could see the reading: 21. "Coming in now?"

It had taken a little convincing to get Kasey and Jake to the entrance of this new tunnel, but he figured they would follow him in now.

"So let me get this straight. You saw an open wooden door the other side of the hill. You checked on the map to find the door at the other end of the tunnel. And you smashed that one in with a crowbar the day before yesterday?" Kasey asked Peter. "Can't believe you did that."

Neither could he. He'd never done anything like it before. But finding out about his dad not getting the job and being taken out of his school all at once, well, he'd lost it. Yet putting all that frustration and anger into the act of busting down that door had calmed him. Or maybe it was talking to Jake that had calmed him. Whatever, it had worked. He'd biked alone for a long time in the sunshine, then returned home to tell his mom the bad news about his dad's job. He did it nicely, gave her a hug, and told her he understood. Then he'd helped her get the cabin ready for the real estate agent's showing. He'd actually done that: helped her get the cabin ready for a showing. They'd opened all the windows to let air and sun in. It had felt good.

When his dad had come home the next morning, the first thing he'd done was remind Peter about the school change. And he'd said it in a tone of voice that felt harsh and Peter had reacted. "You should've asked me first; we should've talked about it. And you shouldn't have spilled the beans to Jake without my permission." That was all he'd said and even now he felt justified. But it had set his dad off, his mom hadn't stuck up for him, and then fireworks had exploded between all three.

His parents had gone on and on about having no money. Get real, his dad had kept saying. Called him a spoiled boy. How do you think we feel? his mother had bleated. Blah blah blah blah. Somehow, no one appreciated it when Peter pointed out that his dad was spending more on beer than he'd taken away from Peter in allowance.

So Peter went for another bike ride to sweat it all off. He ended up back at the wooden door he'd smashed in front of Jake. There, he felt the pull of that new tunnel. A pull he tried to but just couldn't resist. A new, dark place to escape to, another world. One where his real life, all the stuff at the cabin, disappeared. Just the idea of conquering a new tunnel gave him the same high as his magic tricks: made him feel powerful for a little while. Black magic. A spell whose lock on him he hadn't yet picked.

Peter met Kasey's gaze and lifted his chin. "Yup, I smashed it and then I went back to look at it," he said, "but I didn't do more than reach my arm in with the meter. 'Cause I'd promised Jake I wouldn't go in."

Jake smiled. "And you knew I wouldn't come with you without Kasey along."

"And you wouldn't let me ask Micah and Russell," he said, pointing a playful finger at Kasey. He'd actually wanted to invite those guys, show he wasn't like other weekenders. Micah and Russell weren't so bad, he'd decided.

"I told you, no way!" she said. "They'd just boss us around. This can be our tunnel, the one we discovered," she said, stepping in first.

"And we've promised to double back if the meter goes off," Jake reminded Peter and Kasey.

"Yup."

Jake unfolded Peter's map, found where Peter had circled the new tunnel, and nodded. Peter understood Jake well enough to know that, once all safety considerations were out of the way, he'd be totally stoked to explore a new tunnel. They were pioneers, explorers, a secret underground bike club. He didn't even have to worry about lying to his parents. They were so into their own pain, and their efforts to hide it, that they seemed glad anytime he and Jake announced they were going biking.

Jake wheeled his bike into the tunnel to join Kasey, who had the meter now. Peter followed.

"Houdini would've loved it in here," Peter told his companions as all three adjusted their night-vision goggles.

"Houdini the magician?" Kasey asked.

"Yup. Did you know that Houdini used to teach coal miners how to slow their breathing in case of a cave-in?"

"Really?" Kasey said.

"He figured it might help save lives. Isn't that cool?"

"Peter, we're not half as interested in Houdini as you are and we don't want to hear the word cave-in right now," Jake said.

Fair enough. Peter smiled. He loved the way the goggles made the tunnel glow green. He loved the old, thick wooden arches that reinforced the tunnel every few yards: a feature Micah's tunnel didn't have. He preferred the uneven natural rock walls here to the shotcrete in the other tunnel. Made wall rides more exciting. It also made conversation echo less. The whole feel of this tunnel, he decided, was less sterile.

"This must be one of the older tunnels," Peter said. "I like it. Has more character."

"Character?" Jake started laughing, which got Peter chuckling—until he saw Kasey braking. She lifted an arm like a barrier to make sure no one passed her.

"Our first shaft," she announced in an important voice. "Just where the map said it'd be. Two more to come."

Peter looked at the shaft, noticed marks where water had run freely down its walls, and noted iron eye-hooks high up on the wall. "Think those hooks were for holding lanterns back before they had lights?" he wondered aloud.

"Who knows?" Jake responded "Get a load of the ladder in the shaft. It's wood, not iron. Like you said, this tunnel's older."

"I'll go across first," Kasey said.

She's taking this guide job pretty seriously, Peter

mused. Especially since she hasn't even been in this tunnel before. Never mind, might as well humor her.

Kasey placed a foot on the narrow board of the shaft's frame, against the rough wall. It immediately buckled under her foot and fell down shaft, taking a few rocks and some dirt with it. Luckily, she hadn't put much weight on her foot. Years of water running down the walls and soaking the old wood frame made for rotted wood, Peter thought.

"Yikes," Jake said, grabbing Kasey's elbow to pull her back. "Maybe we should turn around. Things don't seem as stable in here as the other one."

"Turn around?" Peter asked incredulously. "Just because of one sketchy shaft frame? We could jump this shaft if we had to."

Brave words, but in reality, it was too big to jump safely. Peter peered down the square hole. He eyed the ladder disappearing into that strange green darkness. He shuddered to think of miners having to climb up and down there for their shifts, maybe with only candles fastened on top of their helmets for light. That's how they'd done it in the early days, before they had battery lamps and elevators. At least, that's what the book he'd photocopied the map from had said. And the first guys down had carried canaries in little cages instead of oxygen meters. If the canaries conked out, the men knew their number was up unless they could backtrack real fast. Peter was glad he had an oxygen meter instead. Easier on canaries.

He kneeled beside the shaft, then lay on his stomach with his chin hanging over the void so that he could lower the oxygen meter down there with one arm. He was surprised when it didn't beep.

"Peter! What do you think you're doing? You drop that and we're dead!"

Peter pulled his hand up, rolled over, and sat up. "Oops, so sorry. I dropped it. Listen for the thud so we know how deep the shaft goes."

"Very funny," Jake replied. He knew Peter too well. "But don't do that again, okay?"

"Micah says air flow is totally unpredictable," Kasey told them. "Sometimes the beepers beep even when there's a straight, level tunnel between two wide-open entryways. And sometimes there's enough air even when both are blocked. Weird, huh?"

"You never told us that before," Jake objected, frowning.

"No biggie," Peter tried to reassure his worrywart friend. "Okay, about this shaft. I think we need to use climbing rope here." Peter pulled out the fifty-foot rope he'd stuffed in his backpack for emergencies, and handed one end to Jake.

"Like how?" Kasey asked.

"I'm going to try and scoot across the other side of

the frame. I'll put one light step on the frame, then shift most of my weight onto the top rung of the ladder, then take one more light step on the frame to get myself over to the tunnel floor. I'm tying in on this rope and Jake's belaying me in case I fall. Then we'll pull the bikes over. Then I'll belay you. Got it?"

"Wow, good idea," Kasey said.

"Okay," Jake replied. Peter was relieved Jake wasn't going to argue. Truth was, Jake was a keener climber than Peter, and had tons of experience belaying.

Once roped, Peter made like a cat, stepping lightly. This time, the frame's board held. He exhaled in relief as the soles of his shoes touched solid rock again on the far side. No way he wanted to fall down that hole, rope or not.

He, Jake, and Kasey were able to tie the bikes on the rope and pull them over the chasm in no time. Jake's long legs managed to fly from rock floor to ladder to rock floor, without even touching the rotting shaft frame. By the time Kasey had done the same and landed beside Peter, Peter figured they had shaft-crossing down to an art.

"You did great," Peter told Kasey. And she had, even if she'd looked pretty nervous. "And Jake, you really should sign up for the long jump in phys. ed."

"Could've done it on my bike with just a little ramp, you know," Jake said.

"Not. Bike would be a mess if it dropped a mile toward the center of the earth. Never mind what you'd look like."

Kasey laughed.

"Got a point there. So, one shaft down, two to go?" Jake checked.

"You got it. It'd be funny if Micah and Russell were right below us now, biking along their tunnel without a clue that we're overhead jumping the very same shafts."

"We'll invite them next time," Jake suggested.

"Maybe," Kasey said sternly.

They carried on in high spirits, even daring to race alongside one another when the tunnel ran straight and their goggles indicated no obstacles. There were no other shafts for the next twenty minutes.

"Hey Kasey, tell your dad we should hold the Copperton race at nighttime, and give everyone night-vision goggles," Peter joked.

The tunnel must have overheard and thought the comment funny, because it began chuckling, then roaring, then heaving its sides in and out. A shower of fine dust released itself from the ceiling and came down on them.

"An earthquake!" Peter shouted, screeching to a halt and covering his head with his hands, never mind that he had on a helmet. "Tremors, right?" he asked, looking wildly at Kasey, who was calmly turning her goggled eyes to the rock walls that had shuddered just a second before.

"No earthquake," she insisted. "They're called air blasts. Micah says they're nothing to worry about. Happen all the time in here. Used to scare me, too."

"What the heck are air blasts?" Jake asked, arms wrapped around himself.

"They're rockfalls in older, sealed-off parts of the mine. Micah's dad and granddad will tell you how they used to work right through air blasts without hardly lifting their heads. No one ever got killed or injured from one. Not in this mine, anyway. At night, the trembling would wake them up in bed—in the mining-company houses. Weird, huh? You'll get used to them."

Peter tried to take comfort from what Kasey said. He smiled a little shakily at her while wiping sweat-moistened dust from his forehead. "Well," he said, "if Micah says they're no big deal and they don't scare you, I guess we'd better get used to them. That's what we pay our guide the big bucks for."

"You got it," Kasey joked back.

Jake looked less certain, but mumbled, "Micah should know best."

16   Deeper

"Micah should know best," Jake repeated, "but I still think we need to get out of here."

"Why?" Kasey challenged, as if offended someone doubted her guiding. But Jake was beginning to doubt her guiding. She'd been in the tunnels a lot, and she knew stuff from listening to Micah, but she hadn't been in this particular tunnel. He'd been willing to overlook that until the air blast had shaken his confidence.

"When you felt air blasts in Micah's tunnel, did dirt come down on you?" he asked her.

"It's not Micah's tunnel, and, no, because the ceilings are different there," she said impatiently. "They're sprayed with that concrete-like stuff."

"Shotcrete," Jake asserted. "You said air blasts are rockfalls in older parts of the mine, right?"

"Yeah, that's what Micah says," she said defensively in a shaky voice.

"Well maybe the wood-sealed tunnels are the oldest ones, the ones where the rockfalls happen. Maybe that's why Micah only breaks through concrete-block plugs."

He looked about. This was a wood-plugged, damp tunnel without shotcrete finishing.

"Jake's right," Peter spoke up. "Let's get out of here. If this place caved in, it'd be our coffin—one not even Houdini could get out of."

Score one for Peter, Jake thought. For actually agreeing with me.

"Okay," Kasey said in a small, tight voice. She looked up at the ceiling. "It's like half an hour's bike ride back to where we came in, right? Ten minutes to the first shaft and a twenty-minute ride from there?

"Yeah, but I have an idea," Peter said, studying the map. "This shows Micah's tunnel is two stories below us. We could ride back to that first shaft and climb down it to Micah's. If our canary doesn't chirp, it's the better way. We'd get to a safer place lots faster."

Canary? Oh, he meant the oxygen meter. Jake could see the logic of Peter's suggestion, but he shivered at the notion of doing a one-handed crawl down an untested wooden ladder to an unsure destination—while the other hand gripped a bike. Still, a safer tunnel sounded really good right now. And just ten minutes away. "Who goes first?"

"I'll lead," Peter insisted.

Kasey said nothing, just fell in behind him. Elbows tucked in, the three BMXers rode in silence, reaching the shaft in record time.

"I'll go first," Peter offered. "Don't start down till I yell up that it's safe."

"Rope yourself up first," Jake suggested, and Peter nodded. So Jake belayed him as he placed a foot on the first rung of the ladder. He and Kasey watched as Peter gripped hard, then reached out to clamp his other hand around his bike's handlebars.

"Good thing we're BMXing and not mountain biking in here, huh?" Peter said.

"We'd be leaving those behind," Jake stated, trying to fathom a one-handed grip on a fifty-pound bike.

"Speak for yourself," Peter answered as he disappeared, a green glow-worm on a rope, creeping down its wormhole.

Jake waited, listening for the oxygen meter's alarm above the sound of Peter's grunts and the banging of his bike against the ladder. He thought he heard a thud, a curse, then silence, and finally a scraping sort of noise. But as he was about to call down to ask what was going on, a loud creak like rusty hinges opening was followed by Peter's joyous shout, "Bingo! Come on down! I'm untying, Jake. You guys don't need to rope up."

Jake heaved a sigh of relief. Kasey helped him pull up the slack rope and stash it back in his backpack.

"Ladies first," Jake said, directing his hands toward the ladder and smiling at Kasey in hopes that would make her stop clasping and unclasping her hands.

"Okay," she said, moving her bike near the ladder and placing a foot gingerly on its first rung. Minutes later, she shouted up, "It's easy, Jake. Come on down." Her voice sounded like it was coming from the other end of a long pipe.

Jake donned his backpack. Then, bike dangling from one hand where he could drop it in an emergency, he made like an ant backing down its burrow—except that ants carry loads twice their own weight. On the way down, he passed a propped-open steel trap door, which seemed to explain the noises he'd heard.

"I picked the lock to open it," Peter spoke proudly from where he stood ten feet below. "Good thing you're traveling with a Houdini, hey?"

Jake shook his head in amazement as Peter's arm shot out from the dark ready to guide him the last few feet to solid footing—if a metal grate can be called solid footing.

"Hey, you guys put in the grate like you said you

would," he said to Kasey. "Right over the old rails. Now we can bike over this shaft instead of carry around it."

"That's right," Kasey said proudly in a relaxed voice. "You wouldn't believe how heavy that was to get in here. But we did it. Too bad Russell only found one. It'd be nice to have them over all the shafts."

The three rolled their bikes away from the grate. Jake glanced at the tunnel's smooth, shotcrete walls and ceiling.

"Were you really dissing shotcrete a little while ago?" he asked Peter. "It's good stuff, really. Forget tunnels with 'character.'"

"Yeah, I feel way safer here," Kasey said.

"Me too," Peter agreed.

Jake glanced back toward the shaft. "So if we'd lost our footing on the ladder, we wouldn't have fallen a mile. But the map doesn't show anything about locked steel trap doors in the shafts."

"Maybe they got put in when the mine bosses sealed off the upper tunnels," Kasey said.

"Makes sense. Shouldn't we close the trap door again?" Jake asked.

"I guess," Peter responded. "After we have a snack."

"Okay, a snack," Jake agreed, suddenly realizing how hungry he was.

They pulled water bottles and chocolate bars out of their backpacks and sat down on the hard floor. The wall's cool dampness felt good against Jake's sweaty T-shirt back. The night-vision-green contours of the dark tunnel calmed him. He wiped dust from the lenses and looked down the tunnel, surprised how light it was. Light? Make that lights, getting brighter by the second. As the sound of gravel crunching under tires reached his ears, he scrambled to his feet. Peter and Kasey rose with him.

"Micah," Peter whispered.

The bikes slowed, drew abreast, and stopped.

"No way," bellowed a familiar, deep voice. Micah shook his head and stared. "Where did you get night-vision goggles, and what part of my order to stay out of here did you not understand?" Then he seemed to notice Kasey, who was half hiding behind Peter. "Kasey Lowe!" he growled.

Peter stepped forward. "Hi, Micah. Hi, Russell. Nice to see you. Kasey loaned us the night-vision goggles, and I wouldn't have come in here without an oxygen meter, which I ordered from the Internet." He held up the meter like some kind of peace offering.

Nice try, Jake thought to himself, but I think it's going to take more than that to get a "nice to see you; won't you join us" out of Micah.

"You—loaned—them—night-vision—goggles?"

Micah said in a stormy voice, turning his black eye-pieces on Kasey. "And brought these guys in here?"

Good thing no one could see Micah's eyes under his goggles right now, Jake thought, because they were probably flashing fire.

Kasey pulled herself up tall, removed her helmet, and shook her bushy hair. "Yes, Micah. I borrowed two pairs. Should've asked Russell first, I know." She turned her face to Russell for a moment. "They're Russell's, not yours. And I can choose my own friends, and invite them anywhere I want, can't I?"

Hey, Jake thought. Kasey's standing up for herself, defying the local leader, breaking down the locals-versus-weekenders custom. He was impressed. But Micah seemed not to be.

"You're a traitor!" he shouted. "You're a bee-yatch. I knew we couldn't trust you. You know nothing about this place. It's dangerous! And what if they"—he jabbed a finger at Jake and Peter—"tell someone about the tunnels, or about us? You can't trust week-enders."

"Yes, you can," Peter interjected. "Micah, calm down. We're not telling anyone, and we were just on our way out of here. Let's just all bike together. Why not lead us all? It'd be safer, huh?"

"Micah," Russell cut off his friend before he could respond. He moved his bike up even with Micah's and looked at him. "We have to get out of here, all of us. You can argue this out later, but not here, not now." He turned to Jake, Peter, and Kasey. "Micah and I turned around back there because the oxygen meter alarm went off. That's never happened to us in this tunnel before. Micah thinks we should get out."

Jake saw Micah move closer to the shaft with the grate and lift his eyes. His goggles must've picked out the propped-open trap door high above, because he seemed to freeze in surprise, mouth slightly open.

Jake was about to tell the group how they had come to be here when the tunnel began to shudder again. A big shudder. Way bigger than before. Instinctively, he and Peter put their backs to the wall. Micah backed off the grill, mouth still open. Kasey put her helmet back on, and Russell was staring at Micah as if waiting for orders when the rocks started coming down. Not from the ceiling, Jake noticed as he put his hands over his helmeted head and crouched down. No, rocks were raining down the shaft, past the still-open trap door, and piling up on the new grate. As the air blast continued and an increasing number of stones started rolling off the grate's growing heap, all five BMXers backed well away from the shaft. Dust filled the tunnel and soon had everyone coughing.

Moving his hands from the top of his helmet to his

ears, Jake tried to muffle the continuous roar, which was spilling tons of rocks down the chute like ice from an ice machine gone mad.

What if we were still up there, Jake thought with throat and stomach clenched. When finally the avalanche ended, the noise and shaking faded, and the dust settled, all five riders stared at one another. They wiped dust from their goggle lenses and dirt from their sweat-dampened lower faces.

"It's totally blocked the tunnel," Russell shouted, jabbing a thumb toward the new floor-to-ceiling rock pile that covered the grill.

Jake was horrified to see that Russell was right. And no one needed to point out the extreme danger and futility of trying to pull rocks out of the barrier to get beyond it.

"What're we going to do now?" Kasey screamed.

"Was that trap door open before?" Micah roared, looking straight at Peter.

"We were biking in a tunnel above," Jake began, trying to keep the note of panic out of his voice as he stared at the new blockade.

"A tunnel above?" Micah roared even louder.

"And an air blast scared us," Peter picked up the story. "It was just a little dirt falling from the ceiling, but we got nervous and decided to come down the shaft and get out through your tunnel. The map showed we could do it, and our oxygen meter said it was safe," he finished, holding the map and meter out toward Micah.

Jake grabbed the meter away from Peter to look at it. "Still okay, but only 20 percent." He addressed Micah. "Why would yours go off down there?" With his back to the blockade, he pointed down the tunnel.

"You picked the lock on the trap door?" Micah said, seemingly to himself, as he raised his goggle eyes to the top of the shaft's new rock pillar. "You may be a Houdini, Peter, but opening up that trap door would've messed with the air flow. Could've created an oxygen-deficient pocket." He picked up a small rock that had rolled to his shoes, studied it, looked at Peter, and placed it in his shorts pocket.

"What are we going to do now?" Kasey demanded again in a shrill voice. "We have to get out of here."

17   Snakes and Ladders

There was, of course, only one thing they could do: bike away from the blockade and hope the beepers didn't go off.

Russell was right about saving arguments till later, Jake knew. Micah, Peter, and Kasey seemed to understand, too. Micah had whirled around to lead the pack in the direction from which his group had come, without saying another word.

Jake biked beside Russell, his head all but spinning from what had just gone down. Here they were, all biking together as one large group at last, but it felt more like a group of fleeing refugees than one big happy family.

"Where did your beeper go off?" Jake asked Russell.

"Just before the second shaft," he said grimly. "So we turned around and were heading back out till we ran into you."

"Let's hope no rocks have come down the second shaft," Jake murmured.

"They'd just keep dropping, 'cause we haven't put a grill across that one yet," Russell responded. "Unless it has a steel trap door above it, too. Hopefully strong enough to hold whatever's come down."

Jake nodded soberly and they rode in silence for a few minutes until Russell turned his head and said in a low voice, "I don't mind Kasey giving you the goggles, even if she should've asked."

Jake, noting that neither Kasey nor Micah was close enough to hear, said, "Thanks."

They rode in silence for a while, concentrating on keeping up with the bikers ahead. Jake braked when they stopped short of the second shaft. To his relief, there was no sign of an avalanche here. If any rocks had tumbled down from above, they were caught on top of a trap door he couldn't see, or they had kept on dropping down to the center of the earth. He watched both Micah and Peter check their oxygen meters like synchronized race officials with stopwatches.

"Still good," Micah reported. He dismounted, grabbed iron handholds sunk into the wall over the ladder, and crossed the shaft in a flash. But as he moved to make way for Peter to join him, the startling beep of the alarm rang through the tunnel.

Micah recrossed the gap so fast he was just a green

blur in Jake's sights. Jake shivered and looked up, then down, the shaft.

"I'll cross it and keep riding while holding my breath, till the alarm lets up," Peter offered. "Then we'll know how long the pocket is. I can hold my breath for a really long time."

"No!" Micah ordered in a commando voice.

It didn't surprise Jake to see Peter step onto the shaft's frame anyway, but this time, Jake leaped forward, pulled him back, and tackled him to the ground. When Jake raised his head, he was astonished to see that Russell had joined in on the tackle. As the two continued to sit on a protesting Peter, they exchanged small smiles. Then they raised their faces to Micah and Kasey, where Jake detected approving smirks.

"I'll climb up the shaft with the meter and see if the way is clear," Russell spoke up.

"No!" Micah objected again, his tone giving way to surprise when Russell grabbed Micah's meter and scrambled up the ladder anyway.

"We've run out of other options," Jake addressed Micah in a quiet voice. Micah didn't reply, perhaps wrestling with concern for Russell, or surprise that Russell was capable of disobeying him.

Instead of a beep, the group below heard Russell's knuckles rapping on something metal. A few seconds later, he dropped back onto the ground beside them.

"Locked trap door. But doesn't sound like it's loaded with rocks on top."

"You don't know that!" Micah said.

"I do, 'cause it sort of echoed when I rapped on it," Russell said evenly.

Peter leaped to his feet. "I'll unlock it," he declared in a voice that seemed to dare anyone to try and stop him this time.

"Houdini to the rescue," Jake muttered with a smile. Jake listened intently after Peter had climbed out of sight. Scrape, scrape, click. That sounded like a lock opening, Jake thought with relief. Creak, grunt. More grunting. Louder grunting, and finally Peter's strained voice.

"Can't … lift it up … far enough. Must … be … a rock wedged above it."

"Let it go, then!" Micah barked.

This prompted Russell to spring onto the ladder and disappear into the darkness. The group heard a mumbled conversation, then a guttural moan from Peter's lips that sounded like he was free-lifting a 200-pound barbell over his head in the gym.

"What's happening?" Jake called up.

No answer. The group in the tunnel waited for an excruciating two or three minutes, until the welcome screech of turning hinges sounded.

"Come on up, folks," Peter's voice called down

victoriously. "Russell's like a snake. He slithered through the little crack I was holding open. He found a big stone that wouldn't let me lift the door, so he had to carry it all the way up the ladder. Our meters are giving us the all-clear."

"Snakes and ladders," Jake mused to no one in particular.

Micah grunted, then grabbed his bike by the handlebars and disappeared up the shaft. "Wait till I check that it's safe," he ordered Jake and Kasey.

He reappeared a few minutes later without his bike and ferried first Russell's, then Peter's, then Jake's, then Kasey's bike up. "Next," he called down like a gym teacher ordering phys. ed. students to climb a rope.

Jake helped Kasey onto the ladder. He watched her inch her way up it, her whole body rigid with tension. That left Jake standing alone in the silent tunnel, toes on the edge of the shaft, shivering, but not from cold.

"Okay, Jake," Kasey called down in a voice that sounded less tense.

Jake shot up in record time. Peter gave him a final hand up. Jake scanned the tunnel quickly. He saw Russell seated on a rock the size of a volleyball—the one that had blocked the trap door. Had he really carried that up the ladder? Jake saw only a few rocks scattered about, although a thick carpet of dirt caked the floor as if the cleaning lady hadn't been around for a while. He watched Peter, Micah, Russell, and Kasey mount and point their bikes away from the shaft as if someone had announced, "Riders ready. Watch the lights."

"One more shaft to cross," Peter declared confidently.

Scowling, Micah pulled that stone out of his shorts pocket, rolled it around his palm like it was some kind of crystal ball, then pocketed it again. "Let's go!" he directed.

They rode hard, Peter and Micah pretending not to be jockeying for the lead. Kasey rode near Jake and Russell, everyone saving their breath to ensure they sped toward the exit as fast as conditions would allow. Not for one second did Jake forget that they were riding in an old tunnel subject to air blasts, blasts that could rain rocks on their heads at any moment. But unlike the shotcrete tunnel two stories beneath them, this one was playing no oxygen games. The meters remained silent.

Once again, it was the screech of brakes that signaled they'd reached a shaft. Shaft No. 3.

"No way!" Micah cried out in distress.

Jake pushed his bike to the edge of the shaft.

"A double," Micah said. "Made for two cages. Must be twenty feet across. But it's only a single shaft down in our tunnel."

Jake noticed water stains running down all four sides.

Peter shrugged as if he ran across double-wide mining shafts every day. "So half of it ends somewhere below us and the other half carries on. At least it's not blocked, and no meters are ringing. Should we go back down to your tunnel or carry on in here?"

Micah lifted a foot and tested the wood frame. It crumbled on him the same way the first shaft's frame had on Kasey. Too much water over the years. Micah accepted the rope Peter produced. Peter and Jake set up a belay for him within seconds. Protected now, Micah stepped further out on the frame while trying to shift some of his weight onto the ladder. But the frame gave way so fast that it pitched Micah into the black hole until the rope stopped his fall. Worse, the oxygen meter on his belt started beeping.

Jake's breath stopped the same way Frodo's must have in the movie *The Lord of the Rings* when Gandalf was clinging to the end of the bridge. Kasey's hand flew up to cover her mouth, which released a whimper.

It took awhile for Jake and Peter to haul Micah back up over the lip of the shaft. The beeper stopped as suddenly as it had started. Jake was glad to see Micah was still breathing, even if it was fast and half-panicked.

"Dampness," Micah said when he'd calmed down, in answer to a question no one had asked. "The walls of this shaft are really wet. Even slight changes in moisture levels can create oxygen deficiency in these tunnels."

Silence reigned.

Slowly, the five riders lined up, their toes just back from the shaft's rotted frame, some staring down, and some across the abyss. Like they were before a freshly dug grave in a cemetery, paying last respects at a funeral.

18   Jake's Jump

It was Kasey who moved first; she sank to the floor and started sobbing. Micah and Russell had turned into statues, still and soundless. Peter dropped to his knees and stared down the shaft as if hoping to see something other than green-black nothingness. Even Houdini seemed stumped.

"Twenty feet across the shaft," Jake said, scanning the walls and ceiling slowly and feeling confidence rise. "Okay guys, we're fine. I've got it."

Four faces turned his way. "Micah," Jake continued, "hand me that rope, and Peter, let me have the shovel you brought."

Jake watched Micah wriggle out of the belay rope and Peter fish out the avalanche shovel with detachable handle they'd packed for emergencies.

"Anyone else have rope?" Jake asked.

Micah dropped his pack, searched inside it, and

handed Jake a climbing rope about the same length as Peter's: fifty feet.

"Russell, if you stand on Micah's shoulders, can you thread both of these through that iron eye-hook high up on the wall next to the shaft? Then tie Micah's carabiner onto one of them?"

"What are you up to?" Micah asked Jake gruffly, but when Jake replied only, "You'll see," Micah handed Russell his carabiner, cupped his hands together, and gave Russell's feet a lift up. Russell pulled the ropes through the hook as if he was an elf decorating a Christmas tree, and leaped down lightly.

"Jake," Peter spoke up in a warning tone as if he'd caught on, "I can tackle you to the ground way better than you tackled me."

"You've done your bit unlocking the trap door," Jake stated. "It's my turn. I know what I can do." He bent down and inserted the shovel between the tunnel floor and its thick layer of dirt. When the others saw what he was doing, they got down on their hands and knees and used their fingers like claws to help scrape dirt into a packed-down launch ramp several feet high. Jake studied the way the tunnel's ten-foot-high ceilings gave way to no ceiling or floor over the double-wide shaft. He studied each side of the shaft carefully, measuring with his eyes, considering.

Now Jake turned and gave instructions to Russell,

whom he trusted more than the others to follow directions without argument. Then Jake looked at Peter, who seemed to be biting his tongue. He ignored Kasey's voice pleading with Micah to stop him. Micah detached his oxygen meter from his belt. Wordlessly, Micah clipped the meter onto Jake's belt, as if passing the baton in a relay race. Then he straightened up and pulled his stone from his pocket. He stared at Jake while gripping his stone as if trying to squeeze water from it. Did he think it was a good luck charm?

Jake rode his bike back as far as he needed to, hands moist and heart hammering, but head clear. Four people's lives depended on his landing this twenty-foot jump—twenty feet across a shaft with no visible top or bottom to where the tunnel started again on the other side. He had to clear it before the shuddering started up again, before rocks started falling. He knew he could do it. He knew he must.

Three, two, one. Never had he cranked his pedals as hard. Never had he concentrated so hard on lifting off a ramp and turning himself into an aerodynamic missile. He tucked his head forward, not wishing it to touch the tunnel's ceiling after he crossed the shaft's roofless airspace. He leaned and breathed, leaned and breathed, felt himself pass the peak of his arc. He commanded the dark runway on the far side—dark but outlined by ghostly green lines—to rise and meet him. He did not look down at the unblinking, perhaps unending, airless hole beneath.

It wasn't a perfect landing; he bumped and bounced and slid while trying to avoid some stones in his path. But his heart soared as his bike slowed. He'd done it.

He turned around to see Micah shaking his head, stone still clenched in his hand. Peter and Kasey were clapping, the echo of their hands implying a stadium of cheering fans. Meanwhile, Russell was winding up like a pro-baseball pitcher with a stone of his own. A second later, Jake heard the whiz of his flying rock: one around which Russell had tied the ends of the two ropes as instructed.

"Home run," Jake called with a thumbs-up as the stone clattered near his feet. He scooped up the stone and leaned his bike against the wall beside the shaft. He stood on his bike seat to thread the eye-hook high up on the wall of his side of the shaft. Then he tied off one of the ropes to the nearest iron bolt he could find. Russell did the same on his side.

Now the four on the far side worked together to hang their bikes from the carabiner on the unanchored rope and send them over to Jake, one at a time. Almost as good as a ski lift converted to carry mountain bikes in summer, Jake decided.

"Nice. Now I've got five bikes. See y'all later," Jake

joked loudly enough for them to hear. If anyone chuckled, he couldn't hear it across the double shaft. All he could hear was the tunnel's spooky echo: "See y'all later."

Peter made the first crossing, hand-over-hand on the anchored rope. Russell had tied a loop in the second rope, a loop that encircled Peter under his armpits like a lasso. This allowed Jake and Micah, whose strong arms had taken charge of the moving rope on either side, to belay Peter almost as they would have in a climbing gym. It was his safety line, his backup.

Russell was the second to cross, his monkey arms and skinny body making short work of the exercise. Probably practiced it all the time somewhere on the empty army base, Jake mused.

Jake was worried about Kasey, who was third up. She swung out over the hole with stiff limbs and a tightened face. Then, to his relief, she started doing the hand-over-hand in a more relaxed rhythm. So he wasn't totally prepared when, on one of her last swings, she missed her grip and fell. The yank pulled Jake close to the edge of the shaft, but his anchor rope held. Kasey now hung in her lasso several feet below the rope she'd been traveling along. Her dangling feet were even with the tunnel floor, but still over air; her life was now dependent on Micah's and Jake's grips. The rope she was on ran from the two boys' hands straight up through the eye-hooks, and down to her lasso, like a giant "M" hung from the tunnel walls either side of the shaft. As Micah and Jake pulled to lift the sagging "V" into something more like a dash, Peter reached over to help pull her to land.

"I almost fell! I almost fell!" she cried.

"You're fine. You were in good hands. You did great most of the way. Could've happened to any of us," Peter reassured her. "Quiet now, so you don't rattle Micah."

"Rattle Micah?" she chimed in with the tunnel's echo. "Impossible."

Micah, being the last one, had to do things differently. Jake hoped Russell had coached him properly. First, he slipped into the lasso and leaped up to grab the anchored rope with his powerful body. Then he came hand-over-hand like a seasoned member of the Marine Corps as Jake and Peter kept his belay rope tight from one side only. Had Micah fallen like Kasey, he'd have dropped farther and swung like a weight on a wound-up pendulum. But assuming Jake and Peter maintained their tight grip, he would have lived. Of course, nothing of the kind happened. Micah was as strong and determined an athlete as Jake had met.

"Too bad we have to leave Peter's rope behind," Micah said as he reached the far side and began looping up his rope to return it to his pack.

"No loss, considering," Jake replied soberly. "Let's hope no one ever needs to use it again."

"Guys," Kasey said, "we're not out yet, you know."

No one needed further encouragement to hop on their bikes and tear down the dark corridor. The five raced in a pack like a sponsored team until black became gray and night-vision green exploded into blinding white light.

Five sets of hands reached up to tear off goggles; five dusty BMX bikes dropped to the grass on the hill. Four weary bodies collapsed onto the grass and raised their faces to the sun. But Micah remained standing, hands balled into fists, face hardened, like a lone knotted tree casting a shadow on the hill.

"Peter," he said in a voice with an edge to it, "want to know the difference between tunnels plugged by concrete blocks and tunnels plugged by wood?"

"Actually, I think we've got that one figured," Peter replied in a wary voice.

"You think?" Micah raised his voice. "First you nearly suffocate us by opening a trap door. Then you trap us by not closing it in time. Then you put Russell in danger by encouraging him to climb through one."

"No one put me in danger!" Russell objected.

"As if that's not enough," Micah continued, "now our tunnel's wrecked. For good. By outsiders who had no right to be in there at all."

"We can find a new tunnel," Russell suggested a little too quickly.

"Micah," Kasey said. "If Peter hadn't opened the first trap door, the three of us might've been killed by falling rocks. And if Peter hadn't opened the second one, we'd all have been stuck in your tunnel forever."

"Who asked you?" Micah stormed. "You're the one who showed 'em in there in the first place. Whose team do you think you're on?"

"Micah," Peter said calmly from where he remained on the grass. "There don't need to be teams around here. I should've closed that trap door sooner, yes. We shouldn't have gone into an older tunnel, true. It's lousy that your tunnel is wrecked. But we've all been trespassing and taking risks. For what?"

Micah's face darkened and he pointed a finger at Peter. "You've got nothing figured. You're a stuck-up rich kid. Is that what they teach you in private school, picking locks? Did you steal your racing bike from somebody or did Mommy and Daddy buy it for you with the same wad that paid for their BMW?"

He kicked a rock in front of him, picked up his bike, and climbed onto it.

Jake watched Peter jump up and place a hand firmly on Micah's front handlebars.

"A stuck-up rich kid," Peter said softly, nodding his head like he agreed. "Except that both my parents are unemployed, our cabin and BMW are for sale, Dad's yanked me out of my school, and I'm about to put my racing bike up for sale. But you knew some of that already, didn't you, Micah? You just need to hear me say that my dad's an unemployed drunk and it sucks." He paused, moving his face closer to Micah's. "It sucks, doesn't it?" he asked so quietly that Jake could barely hear him.

Micah moved his face back from Peter's and let his bike drop to the grass. He stood there looking from one rider to another, as if out of words.

"We all know," Peter went on in a quiet but firm voice, "that these tunnels are dangerous. Why else would they be plugged up? The tunnels were danger- ous even when your dad and granddad worked in 'em, Micah. They're more dangerous now. Me, I'm not trusting my luck again."

To Jake's surprise, that seemed to propel Micah back toward Peter. He stood tall in front of him and pulled that rock out of his pants pocket like someone had just reminded him it was there. He turned it over and over in his hand, up close to his eye, like a jeweler. Finally, he lowered it.

"You know why I ride in the tunnels?" he asked Peter, his voice low with a slight tremor.

"Same reason as me," Peter said quietly. "To get away from your dad. To take your mind off the fact your dad's not working, and that things aren't so great in Copperton."

Jake let his breath out slowly. Had Peter really said that? He half expected Micah's rock-filled hand to rise and strike Peter. He readied himself to jump between them.

But Micah just held the rock up closer to Peter. "Yeah, maybe that too. But this rock, this rock can change things." A tentative smile was working its way onto his face. Jake wondered if he'd ever seen Micah smile before, a real smile, not a sardonic or evil one.

"This rock fell down from your trap door. Look carefully. What do you see?"

The entire group stood and pressed closer for a look. The rock had a metallic luster. It was a shine that reflected off the goggles lying on the grass.

"It's shiny and gold," Peter observed. "Pyrite, right? Also known as fool's gold."

Micah smiled. "No, chalcopyrite, a copper mineral. Might get them to reopen the mines." Jake looked at Russell and Kasey in turn. They looked as surprised as Peter. So Micah had been on a mission, maybe still was on a mission. A mission that took him to dangerous zones.

"They'd consider reopening the mine based on one rock?" Kasey asked quietly.

Micah shook his head. "No, they'd need a stretch of this, and I've narrowed down where to find it."

"Narrowed down, like how?" Jake asked.

"I hang out in the library," Micah said, a defensive tone creeping into his voice. "And I talk to the old-timers."

"Does anyone know you go into the tunnels?" Jake asked.

"No one, not even my dad."

"We could help you," Kasey spoke up.

"I'm good at library research," Jake offered.

"I could help with talking to people in town," Russell suggested.

Micah looked from one to the other while clutching his rock.

"Micah," Peter said, "why don't you come up to the lake? Kasey and Russell too. We'll go for a swim, cool off, clean up, raid my mom's fridge—and discuss this when the parental units are out."

"Okay," Micah agreed after a moment's hesitation. And his smile came to life.

19   Into the Darkness

J ake loved the tickle of a breeze against his face as he and his bike soared into the air above the dirt jumps. His heart leaped as he let go of the bike to soar no-handed, no-footed for a second. For just that exuberant split second, he was a starfish floating in the sky, a spread-eagled human being above an unpiloted, flying bike. Then, just as cleanly, he returned his hands to the handlebars, his feet to the pedals. His bike cooperated like a horse awaiting his master's whistle. The bike's wheels touched down lightly on the far side of the dirt jump. It was a perfect "nothing."

"Pretty sweet, eh?" he called out to Peter, who was lying on some grass nearby, soaking up the sun. A couple of bright yellow wild flowers were poking up beside him. Amazing, flowers on the old mine site. Peter was examining something dangling from his fingers. A caterpillar?

"Sweet," Peter called back, although Jake wasn't sure he'd seen the trick at all.

"Hi, Jake. Nice 'nothing,'" Kasey complimented him as she drew close. "Hi, Peter. What've you got there?"

Jake watched Peter scramble up and grin as Kasey removed her sunglasses.

"Kasey, what're you up to? The guys behind you somewhere?"

"Yeah, but they can't keep up with me," she joked. "So what's that behind your back, Peter? A worm?"

"Nope. Hey, do you like magic tricks?"

Here we go, Jake thought, rolling his eyes.

"I guess," Kasey replied.

"Okay. Hand me your shades."

Kasey smiled, shrugged, and handed over her sunglasses. Peter produced the piece of string he'd been hiding behind his back, put on his biking gloves, and hung her glasses from the string.

"So, I'm going to make your glasses levitate," he told her.

"Uh, you're going to make my glasses float in mid-air? Yeah, right," Kasey said good-naturedly.

Jake watched Peter pull a book of matches from his pocket and strike one. He applied it to the string as Kasey frowned and backed up a step. Whoosh. The string burned up in a second, but the sunglasses stayed exactly where they were, a foot below Peter's gloved hand. Slowly, he steered the hand over to her, the glasses following beneath, and let her snatch them back.

"How the heck did you do that?"

"I soaked the string in salt water overnight. The string burned just now, but the salt crystals held onto the glasses. You just couldn't see them," he replied proudly.

"Hmmm. But don't magicians keep their tricks secret?" Kasey asked in a teasing voice.

"I've been trying to tell him that," said Jake.

"Who's a magician?" Russell asked as he and Micah drew up.

"Peter," Kasey informed them.

"Good, 'cause we're counting on him to pick another lock," Micah replied.

Jake and Peter turned their heads toward Micah.

"We've got a situation," Russell informed them, glancing left and right as if to make certain no one was eavesdropping behind the trees in the bike-jump grove.

"A situation?" Jake echoed, looking from Russell to Micah to Kasey. They didn't look upset or anything.

"Here's how it hangs," Micah began, as the five huddled between the dirt jumps. "Dad got a call from the mine bosses yesterday. An inspector found some of the tunnel plugs 'compromised.'"

Jake watched Peter arch his eyebrows but refrain from interrupting the story.

"Dad asked me if I knew anything about it," he continued.

The group pressed closer to Micah.

"I said I'd been in there with a flashlight a couple of times, but not for a while, because I knew it was dangerous."

"A while—like not since a week ago," Peter said. The others laughed nervously. It was true that none of them had been in the tunnels for a week. The last visit had pretty much freaked them out and Jake for one was glad to be back to the dirt jumps.

"Anyway, he cussed me out good and told me never, ever go in them again."

Total silence greeted that statement.

"And?" Jake coaxed him, fearful of where his need for Peter's lock-picking skills came in.

"And the mine bosses have hired him and a bunch of locals to 'secure' the plugs and tunnels."

"Meaning?" Peter asked.

"Like he was going to tell me anything more than that," Micah said, a smirk on his face. "Anyway, it means we don't have much time now to get everything we need for my report."

"The report that'll get the mine bosses to open up the mine again," Kasey reminded them.

"But the report doesn't mean you have to go into the tunnels again, does it?" Jake asked warily. He didn't like the way this conversation was going. He'd thought Micah had everything he needed.

Micah sighed like a professor forced to explain something in simple terms. "The stuff we've pulled together is great. It's helped me confirm exactly where we need to look to find some really rich samples. Ore samples with chalcopyrite in them. So I know which tunnel to go into, and it's probably the safest one in the whole place."

"Safe," Kasey repeated with a confident smile, looking from Jake to Peter.

"You two don't have to go in, but we three are going. I've wanted to get into this tunnel for a while now. I've suspected it might be the one. But when that chalcopyrite stone rolled over to me just after finding out Peter had picked the lock on that trap door, that's when I got it. That Houdini here could get us through that steel door."

Jake looked at Peter. Peter was nodding and trying to look nonchalant, but Jake could tell he was stoked.

"Sounds good. I'm ready. When do we go?" said Peter.

"Soon as we can. I'm guessing they'll be closing up those tunnels in a few days and we have to get in there before they do."

* * *

Grasshoppers rasped in the grass around them as the boys and Kasey followed Micah on a circuitous route through the rock-strewn hillocks the next day. Vegetation grew sparsely, like stubble on an unshaved chin. Rock-studded dirt, hauled from down deep by miners long ago, struggled to support the bits of greenery. What would it be like, Jake wondered, to be forced to blend in with nature after spending centuries in dark catacombs far beneath the earth? And yet, Jake figured the recovery up here was further along than among the unemployed miners like Micah's father huddled in the dark recesses of Copperton Saloon. Which is why the mine needed to open again and provide lots of jobs.

Micah had decided that today was their day for hitting the tunnels. They'd each told their parents they were going biking to a nearby town and had set off in that direction—in two different groups of course—just in case any parents were watching. Then they'd doubled back to the hills above Copperton, met up, and headed for the mine. As Micah signaled them to slow, Jake found his heart beating just a little faster at the prospect of re-entering the tunnels.

"This tunnel's safe enough to drive your tank through, eh?" Jake kidded Russell.

"That's what Micah says," Russell returned with a smile. "And nowhere near the air-blast tunnels,"

Russell quoted Micah, eyeing Jake as if he was trying to detect a yellow streak.

"Sounds good," Jake declared. It did, really. Anyone who knew how to pronounce "chalcopyrite" had to know which tunnels were safe, he reminded himself. And this trip was going to help save Copperton; it was no joy ride.

He looked about as they neared a rock face. There'd been no sign of anyone since they'd left the road for the hills. So far, so good.

"This is it," Micah announced as he braked and leaned his bike up against a boulder.

Jake stared. Like Micah had said, this time, the entryway was neither timber nor concrete blocks. This time, it was a steel door. Jake dropped his bike and went to rap on it. "Solid," he ruled. "Must weigh a ton." He glanced at the lock. Heavy duty, not like the ones Peter had been playing with.

"We've tried all the skeleton keys my dad keeps in the store," Kasey revealed. "You're our last hope, Peter."

"Well, you came to the right guy," Peter said.

Everyone else moved aside. Micah and Russell stationed themselves as lookouts. Out of habit, Jake timed Peter.

"One minute, fifteen seconds," he informed him as the hinges squealed. He was hardly able to believe his buddy had done it.

"I know," Peter said, hanging his head a little. "I'll try to shave some seconds off next time."

Micah smiled and high-fived Peter as he swung the door open all the way. "You're good," he said.

"You're good, you're good," the tunnel echoed.

When everyone had donned their night-vision goggles and pushed their bikes into the dark, Micah pulled on the door. Everyone jumped as it clanged shut and the bolt clicked back into place. "Locked again," Micah said approvingly.

But he frowned when Kasey started singing.

Into the darkness I descend
The sound of chaos deafening, a blur of foe and
friend
Fire in the sky and on the ground a sea of men
This could be the end …

"Hey, Kasey, nice voice but lousy lyrics," Micah joked.

Jake shivered a little. He watched Micah and Peter check their oxygen meters and give each other an "okay" signal.

"Is there a locked steel door at the other end, too?" Peter asked.

"Affirmative," Russell replied. "We checked yesterday morning."

All the riders but Micah seemed to hesitate. "Everybody ready?" Micah demanded, searching the sculpted rock walls and floor like a building inspector.

"Roger that," Russell piped up.

Micah nodded and took the lead. "Peter, you go last. You've got the other beeper."

Jake preferred the term "oxygen meter." He liked to think its job was to not beep.

They'd biked for ten minutes when Micah paused long enough for everyone to catch up before he took a fork. This one led down so steeply that freewheeling was treacherous. Brakes squealed like bats in the echoing corridor. Around a particularly sharp curve, Kasey rammed Russell and they tumbled to the floor.

"Sorry! Sorry!" Kasey cried as they untangled their bikes from one another.

"It's okay," he replied, helping her up.

When they came to the first shaft, they carried their bikes over it, no problem. Jake was pleased to see that it featured an iron ladder and sturdy bolts on the walls. Afterwards, the group biked on for so long that Jake lost track of time. Sometimes the riders performed tricks, and sometimes they pulled abreast of one another. They crossed the second shaft as smoothly as a well-trained army unit. Jake told himself that meant they were something like halfway between the two doors. They biked maybe another ten minutes. Then Micah halted, checked his map, rode a little farther, and stopped again. He removed his biking gloves and ran a hand over the wall like a fine lady with gloved hands might check for dust. He walked his bike now, goggled eyes shifting from wall to floor. He occasionally picked up rocks from the floor. Soon everyone was doing the same, looking for rocks with that special glint on them, occasionally thrusting one toward Micah for checking.

"That one's good!" he said to Peter, like a father on a beach might compliment a small child presenting him with a seashell.

Soon Micah's backpack was half-full. With a signal, he ushered them back onto their bikes and further along the tunnel.

They'd just followed him around a hairpin turn when Jake felt the tunnel shake ever so slightly. They all piled into one another like racers caught in a Tour de France crash. Not because of the shudder, which was mild and short-lived and seemed to be mostly happening far away. It was because Micah, Jake realized, had come to a dead stop.

"Thought you said we wouldn't feel air blasts?" Kasey accused him, frowning.

Jake and Peter looked at each other when Micah didn't reply right away. Jake breathed easier when Micah turned their way.

"Sorry, I thought we wouldn't. But it's far away. No worries. Let's take a breather." His words were reassuring, but something in his face wasn't, Jake thought.

"Good idea. I'm hungry," Peter announced, unzipping his pack and passing around his mom's home-baked cookies. But when he placed a cookie in Jake's hand, a look passed between them. So even Peter was nervous, Jake thought.

"Micah, what are air blasts exactly?" Jake asked, biting into his cookie. He'd only ever heard about them from Kasey. That was secondhand.

"Old tunnels collapsing," Micah said, licking his lips after his first bite.

"And this one's not old?" Peter asked hurriedly.

Micah shrugged. "Not very. In the old days, they used to build the tunnels right underneath each other. Then regulations made them put more space between them. In other words, more solid rock between the old tunnel's floor and new tunnel's ceiling."

"And ...?" Peter asked as Micah went silent.

"Picture the game of dominoes," Micah said after he'd polished off his cookie. "You line 'em up standing close together. When you knock the first one down, it takes the next one down. And so on until there's a wide enough gap to stop the action. The rest stay standing. Except with tunnels instead of dominoes, we're talking falling rocks, not total collapse."

Jake pictured the oldest, near-surface tunnels aging until they began dropping rocks. The action would shake but not destroy the newer, lower tunnels because the "dominoes" were further apart.

They stood when Micah did and biked a short distance to the third shaft. Once again, they crossed it in record time with no troubles. As they paused to drink from their water bottles, Jake felt relief settle over him. He imagined the steel door now only minutes away. He wiped sweat from his brow and leaned against the rock wall, letting his body relax.

That's when a new rumble started out like low, menacing thunder and he felt the vibration along the length of his spine. Then the thunder boomed overhead, and the tunnel shuddered vigorously. Micah's head jerked up and Jake winced. He didn't like the set of Micah's jaw. Maybe the group wasn't as deep as Micah was claiming?

"Let's get out of here," Peter suggested.

"Yeah," Kasey said, swinging a leg over her bike's crossbar.

"Okay, we've got enough rocks anyway," Micah agreed soberly. But he was slow to climb on his bike, as if he was listening, listening, for something no one else could hear. Russell was studying Micah carefully.

Kasey started singing, probably trying to take everyone's mind off the air blasts, but Micah silenced her. "Shhh, Kasey," he said, staring at the ceiling. Then he got on his bike and took the lead once more.

They headed down the tunnel the same way they'd been going. The dark walls and demanding curves flew by. Jake's heart was racing, even though he kept telling himself they'd be fine. But he'd never been so relieved as when Micah shouted out, "Made it!"

True enough, a steel door loomed ahead.

"All yours, Peter," Micah said, letting him ride to the front. "Let's see your magic show again."

Peter stepped forward to thundering applause. Or rather, to thunder. Once again, the walls around them shivered as somewhere far upstairs, an elderly tunnel coughed. This time, Jake watched a jagged line rip through the ceiling like a pencil-drawn bolt of lightning. Dust trickled ominously from a growing crack in the ceiling.

"Quick!" everyone shouted to Peter at the same time as they ran to throw themselves against the door.

This time, Jake didn't time his buddy, but afterwards he'd swear that Peter's shaking hands accomplished the task in half the previous time. Relief washed over him as the lock clicked back.

"Push!" Micah shouted above the roar of a new roll of thunder.

Sweaty palms pushed hard against cold steel. Slowly, the giant door rotated on its rusty hinges, its screech lost amidst the din. But as everyone piled on top of one another in their scramble to get out, Jake's heart stopped at the sight that confronted them. He fell to his knees screaming "Noooo!"

20 Caverns of Night

"This wasn't here yesterday morning!" Micah screamed. "Russell and I checked!" He pummeled the wall of concrete that stood just a few feet in front of the door until his fists bled. His face was horror-struck. "Someone's only just blocked this door!"

"Someone who discovered holes in a couple of the tunnel plugs," Russell finished for him in a hollow voice as the air blasts above shuddered to a halt. He removed a glove and pushed his index finger against the cement between the blocks. His frown deepened. "Quick-drying mortar. Sets in a few hours. They've beaten us to it," he said, turning toward Micah. Both Micah and Russell turned their faces to the ceiling, as if their goggles had special X-ray qualities that allowed them to see workers many tunnel-stories above. Workers, Peter reflected, led by Micah's father, who thought his son was biking to a nearby town.

Peter let his backpack slide to the ground as he tried to shake himself out of shock. He took some comfort from his meter's reading: still 21 percent. Also, the crack in the ceiling had delivered nothing but a light dusting of dirt. No rocks had fallen.

"It'll take us more than half an hour of hard biking to get back to the door where we came in. Is there any other option?" he asked Micah.

"No," Micah replied reluctantly.

"Then let's go." Russell was already climbing onto his bike.

"Fast," Kasey urged.

"Now!" Peter suggested.

"Now, and that's an order," Micah barked in agreement.

"Order" was an optimistic word for a group of half-panicked BMX racers. They were willing to give Micah the holeshot, so to speak, but after that, it was every rider for himself or herself. Peter hung back to make sure he was the last rider. That way, Micah's meter and his were front and back of the pack to notify them of any "pockets of oxygen deficiency."

The race, of course, was not just against air blasts capable of dropping rocks on their heads. It was also to keep Micah in sight, since only he knew which way to turn when forks in the road flew at them.

Peter felt as if he was on a roller coaster, whipping

around corners at breakneck speed. Being the tail end of the pack didn't feel natural, but at least he'd have plenty of warning before they came to a shaft. Micah's first warning shout was for precisely that: a shaft crossing.

The bikers leaped off their bikes and carried them over the firm frame. This tunnel's one of the safest, one of the safest, Peter kept quoting Micah to himself.

He noticed Kasey struggling a little to keep up with Micah, Russell, and Jake. "Come on. Don't lose Micah," he urged her.

As they carried on, Peter relaxed a little, pretended he was in a real race. He just wished he were on his race bike and up front with Micah and Russell, not in "sweep" position. And that Kasey wasn't forcing him to go slower than he could.

When the third shaft arrived, he and Kasey could barely see the boys ahead of them. Peter felt a kernel of fear in the pit of his stomach. It grew as Kasey nearly dropped her bike down the shaft and moaned like a wounded animal.

"You're fine, Kasey. No air blasts since we've been at this end, and we're almost there. Just try and go a little faster."

She nodded her sweat-soaked face. "I'm trying," she said in a slightly whiney voice.

"Try harder," he said forcefully. He was struggling

to control a rising sense of panic. He dared not sprint past Kasey, but his concern for the growing gap between the frontrunners and the two of them was working its way from his gut to his throat. So, relief flooded him completely when he caught sight of the other boys standing with their bikes beside the door, cheering and waving Peter and Kasey in like spectators at the finish line. But as the two were within a few yards, a jolt knocked Peter right off his bike onto the hard, cold rock floor.

If the previous shudder had been preceded by thunder, this one was delivered with a sonic boom, as if it came from a powerful speaker directly over his head.

He scrabbled on all fours backwards, away from the first small rocks falling from the ceiling between him and the doorway. Through the raised dust, he thought he saw Kasey fall forward toward silhouettes against the door. He also saw his bike lying dust-covered within arm's reach. He lunged forward on his knees to grab it, intending to sprint, crawl, roll, or whatever it took to reach his mates from there. But as more rocks came down between him and them, he instinctively covered his head with his bike, then rolled himself into a ball like a soldier under grenade attack. A giant piece of ceiling came down, missing him by two feet and buckling one wheel of his bike.

He crawled speedily backwards, away from the

falling rock, dragging his wounded bike with him. The light rain of stones now turned into a full-fledged storm. He'd dodged pellets in paintball games, and he'd felt the sting of hailstones before, but nothing ranked with the terror of trying to hide from a meteor shower of bruising rocks. He scrambled deeper into the tunnel, still dragging his bike, small rocks pinging against his helmet as massive chunks of tunnel roof dropped to where he had crouched seconds before.

He wriggled into a crawlspace created by a fallen boulder touching the tunnel wall. He screamed even though he knew no one could hear or rescue him in this chaos. There was nothing to do but sit tight until the cave-in ended. He could only hope, feverishly hope, that the rest of the group had reached the relative safety of the reinforced arch over the steel door. As soon as this rock storm eased, he'd be there to let them out into the light of day.

If he lived through this rockfall, Peter promised himself, he'd never, ever enter the tunnels again. Wood bulkhead, concrete wall, steel door: The boys and Kasey had been fooling themselves that it mattered, fooling themselves that anything down here was safe. His parents would freak if they had any idea where he was. He wished he were biking to that nearby town just the way he'd said he was. The group deserved to be punished for deceiving their parents, even if they had entered this tunnel for a supposedly good cause. But they didn't deserve to die, did they?

Although the tremor ended after a few minutes, it took a long time for Peter's heartbeat and breathing to slow down. He checked his meter: still 21. He checked the tunnel space in front of him: The dust raised was like a heavy fog, but it looked like there was enough room between boulders and rocks for him to make his way toward the door. He felt for his bike. Covered in dust and small rocks, the one wheel slightly buckled, but nothing major.

"Kasey," he screamed. No answer.

As the dust continued to settle, he stood and then stared in growing dismay. The steel door, he figured, should be just a few yards in front of him. But this time, instead of a door that led to a wall, he was facing a solid wall of fallen rocks from floor to ceiling blocking him from the door.

"Jake? Micah? Russell? Kasey?" he cried, voice wavering.

No reply, not even a muffled sound as he leaned against the cave-in's thick wall of rocks. He dared not pull any out in case the deadly pile shifted, finishing off the survivors. Or, he reflected darkly, was no one responding because there were no survivors—except him? Or perhaps—he crossed his fingers—his friends managed to open the door and escape outside.

21　Huddle

J ake leaped off his bike and threw himself into the huddle like a football player going for a tackle. Micah and Russell were standing with mouths open and backs pressed tightly against the steel door, their bikes hugged against their lower bodies like shields. Kasey was the last one in. Jake and Russell reached forward and grabbed her under her armpits even before she'd dismounted, all but dislocating her shoulders to bring her—bike and all—into the huddle.

Jake's screech of "Peter!" was drowned out. The way the ceiling collapsed around them that instant, Jake didn't expect to live. The pounding of the rockfall was deafening, and the dirt raised nearly choked him. He let go of his hold on Kasey to cover his nose and mouth. When the pandemonium finally ended, he heard coughing, felt Kasey step off her bike and move away, and heard her first sob. Then everyone lifted their heads.

"Peter!" Jake screamed again, staring at the wall of debris three feet in front of his face. He pushed his and Kasey's bikes out of the way to lunge forward. He began pulling rocks from the pile, pushing them to the floor, grabbing, pulling, dropping.

"Jake," Micah said as he yanked Jake back by the collar. "You'll make it worse. It's no use. The wall's too thick. Peter's probably okay on the other side. He's got more air than we do."

Jake slumped between the door and the cave-in. A space the size of a small closet held four frightened people and four dusty bikes.

"We need to stay calm," Micah said, placing one hand on Jake's shoulder and the other on Kasey's. "A couple of years ago," he told them in a voice so soft that Jake could barely believe it was Micah, "there was an explosion in a coal mine in Sago, West Virginia. Fourteen guys were buried for forty-one hours in a small space. They took turns using a sledgehammer to try and pound themselves out. They banged on mine bolts so someone would hear them. That made them breathe way harder than if they'd just waited quietly. They finally sat still, sang a little, and wrote letters to their families. One by one, they got dizzy and fell asleep. By the time the rescuers got to them, only one was alive: a guy who'd lain low and taken shallow breaths. I wonder how many more would've lived if they'd sat quietly right from the beginning?"

No one replied. Jake could hear four sets of panicked breathing.

"So let's just save our energy while we take turns trying to unlock the door," Micah added, looking at Jake.

"I have no idea how," Jake said in despair, wiping beads of sweat from his forehead above his goggles. "I don't know how Peter does it, and I don't have the pieces of wire he uses."

At that, Russell bent down and grabbed a spoke from his own bike wheel. He pushed and pulled and bent until he'd freed a piece of wire. He broke it in two and went straight to work on the lock. "If anyone knows how to do this better than me, tell me now."

No one said a thing. The place was stuffy, and getting stuffier by the minute. Micah moved in slow motion to pick up and lean their bikes vertically against a far wall, to give their cell a less crushed feel, to make more elbow room. Jake got down on his hands and knees to examine the bottom of the door, a feat he could barely accomplish in the cramped space. There was no under-door crack, no emergency breathing space—and no way to dig beneath the door.

He took a deep breath, wondering how many more breaths were left in this confined space. He wondered who would collapse first. Wondered if anyone besides Peter could unlock the steel door.

He jumped as a piece of rock flew into the door. It was only Kasey trying to break through it or catch the attention of an imaginary person standing just the other side.

Micah caught and held her wrist before she released the next missile. "The door is steel," he said gently. "That won't even dent it. You're distracting Russell. Save your strength. Save your breath."

Kasey nodded, dropped the rock in her hand, and leaned against the door. There wasn't enough space to sit down. Kasey drank deeply from her water bottle. Then she pulled off her goggles, as if no longer wanting to see anything in the tiny room, in their death trap. She poured a little water into her palm and wiped her dusty face.

There was no sound but for the occasional tap or scrape as Russell worked. Micah stood rod-straight with his oxygen meter cradled in his hands. His goggle-eyes were glued to it.

"How long, you figure?" Jake asked him.

"Don't know," he said evasively, stowing the meter behind his back.

"Yes you do, and we have a right to know," Kasey spoke up.

Russell's hand paused beside the lock.

Micah scanned their cramped space like a work-man about to measure it.

"Twenty minutes?" he said in a tired voice. "It'll beep soon, when it hits 19.5. Don't panic when it does. We won't start feeling breathless till it drops to 17. We'll feel dizzy around 15."

"Then what?" Jake demanded, not sure he really wanted to know.

"We'll start fainting at 9. We'll stop breathing at 6. But someone will open that door before then."

"How long will it take to drop to 6 after the beep?" Jake pressed.

"Impossible to predict. Could be really fast, like that time Peter went up a bad ramp and passed out. Or it could be slow."

Russell's scraping noises sped up. The beeper sounded about fifteen minutes later. Jake thought he could see tears leak from Kasey's eyes.

"I give up," Russell said in a shaken voice. "Someone else needs to try."

The meter's shrill alarm was jarring Jake's nerves. Even before it went off, he'd been fighting a sense of claus-trophobia brought on by a growing breathlessness. He squirmed as he remembered Kasey's earlier comment that everyone in the Copperton group had tried this door numerous times. Even Kasey had tried with all her father's skeleton keys. Everyone seemed to be looking at him.

He turned to face the door and accepted the pieces of wire from Russell. Yikes! Just that small action had him wavering in a first bout of dizziness. He steadied himself against the door and lifted the pieces of wire. He began fiddling, trying in vain to picture Peter's efforts all those times Jake had timed his would-be magician friend. How he wished Peter would break through the rock avalanche right now.

"Listen," he said as he worked. "Peter says you make a little air last by breathing slowly, shallowly. Houdini once lasted ninety minutes inside a coffin that had about twenty minutes of air." Thanks, Peter, for telling me all those stupid Houdini stories. "In fact, Houdini used to teach miners how to slow their breathing. We'll be okay. Think about something that makes you completely relaxed."

That tumble of words left him fighting for air for a second. Now he knew how asthmatics felt.

"Completely relaxed?" Kasey spoke up with bitterness and sarcasm. "While we're slowly smothering to death? When more rocks could fall on us? We're better off scratching notes for our parents on the walls."

"Kasey," Micah said, moving in slow motion to place both his hands gently on her shoulders. "We're not the first ones to be trapped in these tunnels. We may not even be the last. Think about the miners, the brave miners who survived. Think about the forty-six miners trapped for five days underground in Ironwood, Michigan, 1926. Only three died. Forty-three lived. They pooled their sandwiches, ate them crumb by crumb. They sang, tried to conserve their energy. They got rescued." He paused to draw more breath. "Sing for us, Kasey. Please. Just a few lines. Slowly, with shallow breaths if you can."

Kasey, blind without her goggles, nodded in the dark. Jake, who was having no luck with the lock, felt a little of his tension dissipate as she began.

Who's the one who can break the night,
Slay the darkness, and bring forth light?

22 Houdini and Bond

Peter had spotted his damaged bike because its headlight was still working. He crawled forward and detached the light, then trained it on his map of the mine tunnels, which he studied hard. He had to go back to the last shaft. And then he had to climb down, not up. Up was where the air blasts were happening. Air blasts or dynamite. He didn't want to know which right now. The lower tunnels were newer, maybe safer. And if a crew was busy dynamiting and closing off all the tunnel entrances, they'd start from the top and work their way down, right? After all, they hadn't blocked up the door through which the BMXers had entered, the one his friends might have opened and escaped through just minutes ago—at least, the crew hadn't blocked it as of an hour or two ago.

Within a few minutes, he'd formed a plan. It was

a reckless one, but he saw no other way if there was a chance the others were trapped in a small space against the locked steel door. He stood, picked up his bike, and with his gloved hands, unbent his wheel enough to make the bike rideable. Then he returned the bike light back to its holder between the handlebars, climbed onto his pedals, and sprinted to the first shaft. Clutching his bike, he lowered himself onto its ladder, only to be startled by the beep of his oxygen meter. Instinctively, he climbed back up to where the meter went quiet. Then he stared at it as if it was an enemy.

"I can hold my breath for between three and four minutes," he told it. "Just don't beep longer than that."

He took a long, deep breath like a swimmer about to do a high dive. He lowered himself one rung further, one hand wrapped tightly around his bike's throat. The meter's alarm had the effect of a gate call. He descended the rest of the ladder like a one-handed firefighter down a firehouse pole. He leaped onto the floor of the lower tunnel, swung his bike into position, jumped onto it, and tore off into the green darkness. Within seconds, his chest was burning with a desire to breathe. He felt cheated when his oxygen meter continued to beep. No air in this tunnel? That meant, he supposed, that he could open his mouth if he wanted to; it'd be the same thing as holding his breath, right? But he'd been training by holding his breath, and in these scary moments, he preferred to do what felt familiar in order to hold out as long as he could. At least there was no debris, nothing to slow his ride. His heart was pounding in his ears so loudly it almost drowned out the persistent whine of the meter and the sound of his tires against moist, bumpy rock floor. He felt like a burglar being chased after setting off an alarm.

He didn't need to check his watch to know when he'd passed the point of no return. No longer could he turn around, climb back up the shaft, and collapse on the upper tunnel's floor still alive. This was now a race against death, the ultimate test of his lung-capacity training. Maybe the beeper would let up and allow him to gulp air at some point. And what if it didn't? If the map's scale was correct, and if he could keep riding at this pace, and if he could pick a lock in less than sixty seconds—assuming there was a lock and not a concrete-block wall—he had a chance. It was a calculated risk. A risk Houdini wouldn't have hesitated to take.

His lungs were aching when a door came into sight. A locked steel door. In all his practice sessions, never had his chest felt so close to bursting. He leaned the bike against the door, shivered with cold, then felt hot all over. He cursed the meter's continuing shriek; he cursed the way his fingers tingled and shook as he lifted his pieces of wire to the lock. He felt bile in his stomach rise to his throat as the lock seemed to fade and disappear. Where was the lock? It was as if his night-vision goggles had just failed.

"Hypoxia lowers your night vision," his father's voice came to him. "Hot and cold flashes and tingling … only seconds to react."

Peter tore off his useless goggles. He ran his left hand blindly across the door, felt the lock, held onto it tightly. He lifted his wires with his right hand, felt the tingling in his fingers increase, gathered all his concentration. He couldn't stop the waves of nausea; he just had to work through them.

"Jake, I need to break my record. I need to do this in less than sixty seconds," he thought. "Jake, where are you?"

The nausea won. His vomit sprayed all over the door, even as the door gave way. He fell to his knees on top of his bike and heaved some more—gasped, heaved, gasped. He lay with his head in the dirt, his stomach on his bike, his feet still in the tunnel acting as a doorstop, the world spinning around him. A gentle breeze caressed his face.

"Did I beat sixty seconds?" he asked an imaginary Jake beside him. "Jake? Jake!" he remembered.

He sprang weakly to his feet. The door behind him clanged shut. He lifted and jumped back on the bike and began riding, the pieces of wire between palm and bike grip. He rode up the hill, looking, looking. There it was: the steel door he'd unlocked to let them in what seemed days ago. He could hear an oxygen meter beeping inside. His own had gone silent. He dropped his bike and banged on the steel door as he reached up for the lock.

The chorus of shouts this elicited on the other side startled him, thrilled him, panicked him. He inserted the wires, prayed, tried to shave time off his previous record.

Maybe it was his lightheadedness, but this time, before he could pick the lock, he lost his footing and toppled to the ground. Weak and disoriented, he tried to cry out. Next thing he knew, a crowd of medics was crouched beside him, pummeling his chest to revive him, thumping him everywhere. He tried to bring his eyes into focus. The first medic looked a lot like Jake Evans. The others bore an amazing resemblance to Micah, Russell, and Kasey. They weren't administering cardiopulmonary resuscitation, after all. They'd fallen on him as the door had given way from inside. Now they were hugging him.

Peter heard someone yell "grab the bikes." Then he heard the heavy door slam shut, the lock click back into place. "Did I open it?" he asked in a hoarse voice, trying to pull himself up on his elbows.

"No, Peter," Jake said, handing him a water bottle. "I did. From finally remembering roughly how you did it."

Peter gazed at Jake, whose face seemed chalk-white. He turned to look at Micah, Russell, and Kasey, whose faces, though equally drained, seemed happy to see him. His gaze fell to a tangle of dusty bikes lying on the ground behind them.

"What happened to you?" Russell asked. "How'd you get out?"

Peter gave a quick recap of his movements, of his big gamble. As he spoke, he let dribbles of water revive his sore throat.

"You did good," Micah said, shaking his head admiringly. "You did good for a weekender," he qualified that with a grin. "You'd have saved us if Jake hadn't. Our meter went down to 13. You made like Houdini and James Bond put together."

"Like James Bond?" Peter repeated, wetting his dry lips. "Bond, James Bond."

The group jumped as an explosion sounded from uphill. The ground shook as if in the grips of a minor earthquake. Peter joined the others in gazing at the empty hillside hiding a maze of tunnels.

"It's the tunnel crew," Micah said, his face contracted in distress. "My dad's probably leading it. I thought it'd take them a couple of days to organize and do it:

plug up the entryways and dynamite the worst tunnels. We have got to get out of here, now!"

"Because it's dangerous standing out here?" Peter asked dumbly.

"No, because we don't want to get caught!" Micah responded, slapping at his dust-covered clothes and pulling his bike from the heap.

Peter looked from one to another. They'd have a hard time explaining where they'd been. They looked just like miners emerging from an underground shift, dust-covered, sweat-streaked, and raccoon-faced from where their goggles had been. Even the bikes were a mess: Russell's was missing a spoke for some strange reason, and Peter's front tire was still warped.

"The lake," Peter suggested. "We'll ride to the lake and dive in to get the worst of it off. Then we'll use the shower at my cabin, and the garden hose to douse the bikes, and the dryer for our clothes. I'll think up a story if my mom's around."

23 Cleanup

Luckily for the group, neither Laura nor Richard Montpetit were at home that afternoon. A dripping party of five took turns showering, cleaning their bikes, drying their clothes, and raiding the Montpetits' refrigerator and kitchen cupboards.

Laura seemed delighted to find them sitting on the Montpetit dock, drinking lemonade and sharing plates of food, when she returned. "Peter, you're home early! And I had no idea you'd made so many friends in Copperton. Please introduce me."

Jake helped Peter introduce Micah, Russell, and Kasey, and didn't mind one bit when Laura disappeared into the house and reemerged with bowls, freshly washed strawberries, and a carton of ice cream she'd just bought at the store.

"Save some for Richard. He'll be home in a few hours. He actually found some work today, Peter honey."

"Work?" Peter asked, looking as hopeful as Jake felt.

"Not with an airline—not yet," Laura said. "Just a day job with that guy he's been talking about, Sven or something."

Jake worked hard at not looking toward Micah just then. Peter seemed to be doing the same.

"He's a mine manager," Laura continued, "and needed a work crew for the week, starting today. Just grunt work, cleaning up some old mine messes, I think he said. Richard thought it'd be good for him to do something physical and get to know some local people. He'll be hungry and tired tonight, don't you think?" she asked Peter with a smile.

"No doubt," Peter replied. "Funny he didn't mention it at breakfast this morning."

"It was all arranged last-minute. Sven phoned him just after you headed off biking. Then he picked him up in an old pickup truck loaded with wheelbarrows and shovels and other men and whatnot. How was your bike ride, by the way?"

"It was epic, totally interesting, but a bit dusty," Peter replied, as the group all mumbled similar answers, nodding like puppets while exchanging furtive glances.

"Wonderful. Well, you kids are welcome to hang out here. But when your guests have gone, honey, can you and Jake help me? We need to clean up the cabin for a showing tomorrow."

"Absolutely," Peter told his mom as Jake nodded too.

* * *

That evening, after Micah, Russell, and Kasey had gone home, Peter and Jake scrubbed and swept and straightened the house with all the energy one might expect out of two teenage boys who had just had near-death experiences. In the process, they earned special praise from Laura Montpetit. Peter teased his dad about his dusty clothes and increased biceps that evening, without getting much information in response about what he'd been up to all day.

The next day, Laura broke the news that they'd had an offer on the cabin and had accepted it. Jake saw a mixture of relief and sadness in her eyes.

"That's good, Mom," Peter said, his face set, rising from his chair to peck her on the cheek. "Real good. Didn't take so long after all, did it?"

Jake felt his chest expand with pride for Peter. The news had to be a big blow, really.

"We can still come back here and camp sometimes, right? We can do family hikes? Maybe with Jake, too?"

"We sure can," Laura said, hugging her son as she wore a proud smile.

"Mom—and Jake too, since I haven't told you yet, old buddy—guess what I just sold on eBay?"

"You sold something on eBay?" Jake asked.

"What did you sell, honey?" Laura asked.

"My race bike."

"You sold your race bike?" Jake asked.

"Yup. I'm going to put part of the money toward a new wheel for my street bike."

Peter, willing to give up his race bike? He really was coming around to accepting his parents' situation. Good for him.

"I thought that wheel was looking a bit wobbly," his mom said. "You and Jake are always doing tricks that are hard on your poor bikes, aren't you? Well, if you're willing to give up racing until you save up for a race bike again, that sounds like a smart idea, Peter. We all need to stretch our dollars this summer."

"Thanks, Mom. I'm going to buy the new wheel off Kasey's dad," he said decisively.

"Hmmm, guess that makes the Lowes lucky to have a weekender like you in town," Jake teased.

"Wrong. Makes us lucky to have them," Peter ruled. "Hey Jake, let's finish up those projects in the garage."

Laura shook her head and placed her hands on her hips. "Magic-show stuff, right?"

"That's right, Mom. No coming in till we're ready."

"Fine with me," she said, ruffling her son's hair.

In the garage, as Jake held the stopwatch, Peter

managed to unchain and remove his straitjacket by himself on the first try.

"You're the man!" Jake shouted enthusiastically.

"Don't you forget it," Peter replied. "Now I just have to do it faster."

"Keep on practicing, Houdini," Jake said, picking up a saw. "I'm going to see if I can get your coffin finished before supper." Peter, no surprise to Jake, had requested a coffin for his next magic-show trick. So Jake had designed one himself and gathered up the scrap wood he needed to make it. It was coming along, Jake thought, as he finished sawing and began hammering. He just needed to buy some hinges this afternoon to complete it.

"This is going to be my last magic show," Peter informed Jake. "Then I'm giving up magic. Bored with it. Gotta find a new hobby."

"About time," Jake said, straightening and reaching for more nails. "But not before you use this coffin."

"Oh, I'll use it, alright. Highlight of the show. Hey, you know what? Houdini had a brass coffin."

"Well, feel free to buy some brass spray paint," Jake retorted around two nails pinched between his lips.

Peter, who'd freed himself from his chains again, grabbed the phone and dialed.

"Kasey! Hey there. It's Peter. Yeah, I know you're working. That's why I called. I need to buy some spray paint—brass, please. And Jake needs three hinges, maybe two inches long each. Whatever's cheapest … You do? Great! Special delivery, please," he requested, grinning into the phone. And then, "What do you mean, that costs extra?"

"That girl's cheeky," Peter complained. "But she's on her way."

"Perfect," Jake replied.

"Hey guys," Kasey said breathlessly ten minutes later as she pulled up to the garage's open door on her bike and tossed the purchases to Jake's outstretched hands. "Did you hear about Micah?"

"No," Jake said around the screwdriver in his mouth as he readied the coffin for its hinges. Kasey didn't seem to recognize the wooden box on the floor as a coffin, or she'd surely have asked what was going on.

"When he showed his dad the samples and the report he'd started writing, his dad helped him out and drove him to the mine's head office." She hesitated. "That was after his dad chewed him out for getting the samples in the first place. But his dad doesn't know anything about us helping out. He thinks Micah got those samples weeks ago, before he was told to stay out."

"Uh-huh," Peter replied.

"Turns out those rocks had lots of whatever mineral it was that Micah was looking for. And some high-up mine people are coming 'round to do tests now.

So they've stopped Sven and his crew from doing any more tunnel destruction."

"That's good," Jake said.

"They're even talking about reopening a section of the mine. Has to do with the price of copper rising, Micah said. So Micah is some kind of big hero in town. And the mining company is giving him a full-time summer job. He says he's going to swing one for Russell, too."

"A job in the mines?" Jake asked Kasey, happy for them.

"Well, just grunt work, minimum wage. But he's stoked."

"Well, good for Micah," Peter pronounced. "Better than serving ice cream part-time."

"Yup. He won't need a discount at the hardware store any more. Just as well, since my dad has ended that."

"Ended your friends getting discounts there?" Peter asked, frowning. Jake knew he was thinking about the wheel he planned to buy there.

"Yes. I told him to. I figured out he was only doing it to help me make friends. And that's not how to get real friends." She smiled faintly at Jake and Peter, her face reddening. "And I've told him to stop exaggerating about my riding. It's embarrassing. I'm not really all that good."

"But you're going to be," Peter said.

She laughed and shook her hair out of her face. "You got that right!"

"So," Peter mused. "We might've helped get the mine reopened. That totally rocks! Hey, get it? Rocks!"

Jake and Kasey glanced at each other and rolled their eyes.

"Boys!" Peter's mother called to them as she approached the garage. "Oh, and Kasey. Hi, Kasey. Can I come in? You'll never guess what."

Jake instantly crossed his fingers, knowing that Peter's dad was in Seattle today at a job interview.

Peter's head jerked up and he surveyed his mother's face carefully. Jake, seeing the smile that lit up her eyes, relaxed his fingers.

"Yes you can come in. He got it?" Peter asked with a tremor in his voice.

Laura nodded, smiling, and held her arms out for a hug. She looked close to tears of happiness. "He wants to celebrate," she said. As Peter squirmed away, she straightened up and looked at him sternly. "Don't ask about keeping the cabin or going back to your old school. Those decisions aren't reversible."

Peter nodded soberly. "I know. No worries," he said softly, as if he really were okay with that. Almost as if he'd grown up a whole bunch lately, Jake thought.

"He was thinking about us holding a big barbecue, something we could invite his Copperton work-crew mates and their families to, so they could have a good time too," she said, scratching her head.

"What?" Peter asked, tossing a bemused look at Kasey. "Something that would mix locals with week-enders? Never been done, you know. Would never, ever work."

Kasey let loose a vigorous laugh. "Oh, it's been done, although maybe in a sort of underground way."

"I say your dad's got the right idea," Jake spoke up. "It's time people around here stopped seeing each other in those terms. That's too tunnel-visioned."

"So you think we should do it, have a big backyard barbecue here? People could swim in the lake." Laura's eyes were darting around the backyard.

"Absolutely," Jake ruled. "I say it'll be the best event of the summer. We could even bring in some enter-tainers. You know, some BMX bikers performing demo tricks. And a singer." He looked at Kasey, who smiled. "Maybe even a magician who can get himself out of a chained-up coffin."

"A magician? A coffin?" Kasey asked, looking from Peter to Jake as Laura chuckled, spun around, and headed back to the house.

"The one I'm about to spray-paint copper," Jake replied, pointing to his nearly finished creation.

"Copper? But Houdini's was brass," Peter protested.

"Maybe so, but you're not Houdini," Jake replied.

"Not yet, anyway. And I say if we're finally nailing the lid on Copperton's locals-versus-weekenders grudge match, copper's the appropriate shade."

"Brilliant," Peter agreed after a moment's hesitation.

"But you told me to bring brass spray paint," Kasey objected. "It'll cost you extra to exchange that for copper, especially if you're talking another delivery."

"I think not," Peter said, reaching for his straitjacket, donning it, and letting Jake tie it snugly behind his back. Smiling at Kasey, he stepped into the coffin and lowered himself till he sat cross-legged in its middle. "I think you'll do one for free. So, champ, use all that training to race your bike down to the store and back. By the time you return, Jake'll probably be ready to let you lock me up."

He lay down full-length and let Jake drop the lid over him. The soft thud of the newly hinged cover hitting the sides raised a small cloud of sawdust. As Jake pounded nails through the lid into the sides, more sawdust rose to mix with the sweat on his forehead.

Kasey's eyes widened as Jake wrapped lengths of chain around the coffin, and lined up half a dozen locks on a nearby workbench. "But how will he get out?" she asked with distress.

"Magicians never reveal their secrets," came the muffled voice from inside the box. "But just like in mazes, there's always a way out. Always."

Acknowledgements

Of enormous help in the writing of this book was Laura Knowles, an English teacher, two-time BMX provincial champion racer, BMX coach, and mother of BMX racers Russell and Kasey Knowles. Kasey is a three-time Canadian national champion.

Also key in assisting me with this story was Terry Johnson, mine manager of the Britannia Mine Remediation Project in British Columbia, Canada, on which "Copperton Mine" is loosely based. The B.C. Museum of Mining, a national historic site in Britannia, is a popular tourist destination that offers guided tours. (I had my own personal tour with Terry.)

Terry and I would like to make the following points clear:

It is extraordinarily dangerous to go into an abandoned mining tunnel. Trespassers in such tunnels frequently drop dead with no warning due to a lack of oxygen. "Pockets of oxygen deficiency" are very real and very unpredictable. They can occur anywhere, anytime underground, including in spaces that had sufficient oxygen just moments before. Air blasts and rockfalls, although less common in hardrock than soft rock mines, are real. Tunnel plugs can be made of a number of materials, none of which implies that one tunnel is safer than another.

All mining disasters retold by the BMXers are real historic anecdotes. And airplane-pilot training programs have indeed used pencil mazes as part of hypoxia recognition.

Allan and Jesse Jones, BMX racers, were kind enough to read through the manuscript and suggest changes. Ron Mercer, who dubs himself "the oldest surviving freestyle rider in the Vancouver, British Columbia region," is a dedicated BMX teacher who took the time to read the manuscript.

My husband, Steve, and son, Jeremy, both contributed to the plot, while Dr. Martin Blackwell, G.P., advised me on hypoxia.

Most of Kasey's lyrics are taken from the poem "Coal Mines" by Thomas Llewelyn Thomas, published in 1863, and reprinted in *Caverns of Night* by William B. Thesing and Ted Wojtasik. The lyrics beginning with the lines "Who's the one" and "Into the darkness" are reprinted with the bemused permission of Retrofire, www.retrofireband.com.

Of the many books and articles on mining I read, the most helpful was *Cradle to Grave: Life, Work and Death at the Lake Superior Copper Mines* by Larry Lankton (Oxford University Press, 1991).

And as always, there are the following people to thank: my literary agent, Leona Trainer; my editor, Carolyn Bateman; my speaking tours agent, Chris Patrick; and all the staff of Whitecap and Firefly Books.

Arch rivals and sometimes friends Peter and Jake are delighted to be part of a whitewater-rafting trip. But after a series of disasters leaves the group stranded in the wilderness, it's up to them to confront the dangerous rapids to search for help. This is the first title in the extreme outdoor sports series by Pam Withers.

ISBN 978-1-55285-510-2

ISBN 978-1-55285-530-0

Jake, Peter, and Moses are looking forward to heli-skiing and snowboarding in the backcountry near Whistler. But just after they're dropped off on a mountain peak, bad weather closes in and a helicopter crashes. It's up to them to rescue any survivors and overcome avalanches, hypothermia, and wild animals to make their way to safety.

It's summer vacation for best friends Jake and Peter, and when they're invited to help develop a mountain-bike trail west of the Canadian Rockies, they can't believe their luck. But as they start working hard in an isolated park, the boys sense that something's not right. Join the boys as they plunge into the mountain biking descent of their lives.

ISBN 978-1-55285-604-8

ISBN 978-1-55285-647-5

Fifteen-year-old friends Jake and Peter land jobs as skateboarding stuntboys on a movie set. They couldn't be happier, but their dream job proves to be more trouble than they expected. A demanding director, an uneasy relationship with three local skateboarding toughs, and a sabotage attempt are just some of the obstacles they encounter. After a police chase and an accident that lands someone in the hospital, Jake and Peter know it's time to find out who has it in for them, and why!

Jake and Peter find extreme adventure once again. This time a scuba-diving accident leaves the best friends and a surfer girl stranded on a deserted island with surf-boards as their only means of escape. The storm of the century is fast approaching, and the boys need to think fast if they're going to get home in one piece.

ISBN 978-1-55285-718-2

ISBN 978-1-55285-783-0

Jake and Peter stumble upon adrenalin-pumping adventure again, this time high in the peaks of the Bugaboo Mountains, just west of the Canadian Rockies. Jake is obsessed with solo-climbing a soaring granite spire. His best friend Peter is as absorbed with filming Jake for a video as he is in not divulging his secret fear of heights to the runaway girl who joins them.

Best friends Jake and Peter spend the summer as junior guides for a dirt-bike trail outfitter on a remote ranch near Spokane, Washington. They consider themselves the ideal team, but Peter is a freestyle maniac who hates doing bike maintenance and Jake dreams of being a motocross-race mechanic. It takes a series of race mishaps topped off by a natural disaster to convince them that successful dirt bikers understand their motorcycles inside and out.

ISBN 978-1-55285-804-2

ISBN 978-1-55285-856-1

Jake and Peter are junior instructors at a noisy wakeboard school that's attempting to share a remote lake with a community of save-the-earth society dropouts (otherwise known as hippies). When Peter decides to encourage the wild streak in a rebellious hippie girl across the lake, she runs away to hide in a nearby abandoned sawmill, only to discover it's not as abandoned as it looks. Soon, community tensions erupt, and the boys get more action than they bargained for.

10 Stay tuned for the tenth and last book in the Take It to the Xtreme series, when Jake and Peter join a mountain-boarding descent down a picturesque mountain that turns out to be an active volcano. See www.TakeItToTheXtreme.com.

 P am Withers is a keen outdoors person who has been involved with many sports. She served as an editor with *Adventure Travel* magazine in Seattle and New York City before doing stints with the *Seattle Times* and *Seattle Post-Intelligencer*. She wrote for publications ranging from the *New York Times* to *McCall's* before working as a book editor and young-adult novelist.

She has been nominated for numerous awards for both her journalistic and fiction writing. She has also found time to race whitewater kayaks, paddle the Colorado River through the Grand Canyon, camp and kayak through northern Russia, and dabble in climbing, skiing, scuba diving, and snowboarding. She speaks to more than 15,000 children across North America per year, as well as at writers' conferences and parents' groups: www. TakeItToTheXtreme.com. Besides the Take It to the Xtreme series, Pam is author of *Camp Wild*, *Breathless*, and *The Daredevil Club*. She lives in Vancouver, British Columbia, with her husband and teenage son.